Maigret Sets a Trap

GEORGES SIMENON

Maigret Sets a Trap

Translated from the French
by Daphne Woodward

A Helen and Kurt Wolff Book
Harcourt Brace Jovanovich, Inc.
New York

ISBN 0-15-155137-5
Library of Congress Catalog Card Number: 70-182331
Printed in the United States of America

Originally published in French under the title *Maigret Tend un Piège*

B C D E F

Maigret Sets a Trap

1

Commotion at the Quai des Orfèvres

From half past three on, Maigret raised his head every now and then to look at the time. At ten minutes to four he initialed the last page on which he had been making notes, pushed back his chair, mopped his forehead, and threw a hesitant glance at the five pipes lying in the ashtray, which he had smoked without bothering to knock them out afterward. His foot pressed a button on the floor under his desk, and there came a knock at the door. Mopping himself again with an outspread handkerchief, he growled:

"Come in!"

It was Inspector Janvier; like the superintendent, he was in his shirt sleeves, but he still wore his tie, whereas Maigret had taken his off.

"Give this to be typed. Tell them to bring it to me to sign as soon as it's finished. Coméliau has to have it this evening."

This was August 4th. All the windows were open,

but that made the room no cooler, for they let in hot air which seemed to rise up out of the softened asphalt, the scorching stones, and the Seine itself, which one half expected to be steaming like water on a stove.

The taxis and buses on the Pont Saint-Michel were going more slowly than usual, as though dragging along, and it was not only at Police Headquarters that people were in their shirt sleeves; outside on the sidewalks the men were carrying their jackets, and just now Maigret had noticed a few in shorts, as though at the seaside.

There couldn't be more than a quarter of the population left in Paris, and they must all be thinking with equal envy of those who, at this very moment, were lucky enough to be dipping in the little waves or fishing on the shady bank of some peaceful stream.

"Have they arrived, over there?"

"I haven't seen them yet. Lapointe's watching for them."

Maigret rose to his feet, as though with an effort, and selected a pipe which he emptied and proceeded to refill; after which he strolled over to a window and stood there, looking across the river at a certain café-restaurant on the Quai des Grands-Augustins. It had a yellow-painted front. The door was two steps down, and inside there it must be almost as cool as a cellar. The bar was a real, old-fashioned, tin-topped affair, there was a slate hanging on the wall with the menu written on it in chalk, and the place always smelled of calvados.

4

Even some of the booksellers' boxes along the riverside were shut and padlocked!

He stood motionless for four or five minutes, puffing at his pipe, saw a taxi pull up not far from the little restaurant and three men get out and make for the steps. The most familiar of the three figures was Lognon, the inspector from the 18th *arrondissement*, who at this distance looked even smaller and thinner than usual; it was the first time Maigret had seen him wearing a straw hat.

What would the three men drink? Beer, no doubt.

Maigret pushed open the door of the inspectors' room, where there was the same atmosphere of indolence as in the rest of the town.

"The Baron's in the corridor?"

"Been there half an hour, Chief."

"No other journalists?"

"Young Rougin's just arrived."

"Photographers?"

"Only one."

The long corridor of the Criminal Police Headquarters was almost empty too, except for two or three people waiting outside doors to see one or another of Maigret's colleagues. It was at Maigret's request that Bodard, of the Financial Section, had summoned, for four o'clock, the man of whom the papers were talking every day—a certain Max Bernat, unknown a fortnight ago, but now the central figure in the latest financial scandal, in which thousands of millions of francs were at stake.

Maigret had nothing to do with Bernat, and at the present stage of the investigation Bodard had nothing to ask of Maigret. But because Bodard had casually announced that he would be seeing the crook at four o'clock that afternoon, there were at least two gossip-column journalists and a photographer in the corridor. If it got about that Max Bernat was at the Quai des Orfevres, other journalists might turn up, too.

At precisely four o'clock, sounds of a slight commotion reached the inspectors' office, denoting the arrival of the crook, who had been brought from the Santé prison.

Maigret waited for about ten minutes, pacing around the room, smoking his pipe, mopping his forehead from time to time and throwing a glance at the little restaurant on the other side of the Seine. Then he snapped his fingers and said tersely to Janvier:

"Go ahead!"

Janvier went to the telephone and called the restaurant. Lognon must be near the telephone booth, on the lookout, and would say to the proprietor:

"That's surely for me. I'm expecting a call."

Everything went as expected. Maigret, moving a little heavily, feeling rather uneasy, went back to his office. Before sitting down he got himself a glass of water from the faucet.

Ten minutes later a familiar scene was taking place in the corridor. Lognon and another inspector from the 18th, a Corsican called Alfonsi, came slowly up the stairs; between them walked a man who seemed embarrassed and held his hat in front of his face.

The Baron and his fellow journalist Jean Rougin, who were standing outside Superintendent Bodard's door, understood the situation at a glance and sprang forward, while the photographer brought his camera into action.

"Who's that?"

They knew Lognon. They knew the police almost as well as the staff of their own newspapers. If two inspectors belonging, not to Criminal Police Headquarters but to the Montmartre police station, brought a man to the Quai des Orfèvres and the fellow was hiding his face even before he'd caught sight of the journalists, that could only mean one thing.

"Is it for Maigret?"

Lognon made no reply, but went to Maigret's door and knocked softly. The three men disappeared inside and the door closed again.

The Baron and Jean Rougin exchanged glances, like men who had just overheard a State secret; but knowing they were both thinking the same thing they felt no need for comment.

"Got a good one?" Rougin asked the photographer.

"Except that the hat was hiding his face."

"That'll do to start with. Send it off to the paper quickly and come back here. We can't tell when they'll be out."

Alfonsi came out almost at once.

"Who is it?" they asked him.

He looked embarrassed.

"I can't say anything."

"Why not?"

"Orders."

"Where does he come from? Where did you pick him up?"

"Ask Superintendent Maigret."

"A witness?"

"Don't know."

"A new suspect?"

"I promise you I don't know."

"Thanks for being co-operative."

"I suppose if it was the killer you'd have put handcuffs on him?"

Alfonsi went away with the regretful expression of one who would have liked to say more; silence returned to the corridor, and there were no comings or goings for more than half an hour.

Max Bernat, the crook, came out of the Financial Section office, but he had already declined to second place in the interest of the two journalists. As a matter of conscience they put a few questions to Superintendent Bodard.

"Did he give any names?"

"Not yet."

"Does he deny that he was helped by some political figures?"

"He neither denies it nor admits it, he leaves it in doubt."

"When will you be interrogating him again?"

"As soon as certain points have been checked."

Maigret emerged from his office, still in his shirt sleeves and with his collar unbuttoned, and made for the Director's office; he looked preoccupied.

This was another sign: in spite of the holidays, in spite of the heat, Criminal Police Headquarters was preparing for one of those important evenings, and the two reporters remembered how an interrogation had sometimes lasted all night, even gone on for twenty-four hours and more, without anyone being able to discover what was happening behind the closed doors.

The photographer had come back.

"You didn't tell them anything at the office?"

"Only that they were to develop the film and keep the prints handy."

Maigret stayed with the Director for half an hour; then he went back to his office, waving the reporters aside with a weary gesture.

"Tell us, at least, whether this has any connection with . . ."

"I have nothing to say for the moment."

At six o'clock the waiter from the Brasserie Dauphine brought a trayful of mugs of beer. Lucas had been seen to leave his office and go into Maigret's, from where he had not yet emerged. Janvier, with his hat on, had been seen to rush out and jump into a police car.

Something more unusual was that Lognon appeared and went to the Director's office, as Maigret had done.

True, he was there for only ten minutes, after which, instead of leaving the building, he went into the inspectors' office.

"Did you notice something?" the Baron asked his colleague.

"His straw hat, when he first arrived?"

It was difficult to imagine the Gloomy Inspector, as everyone in the police and the press used to call him, wearing an almost jaunty straw hat.

"More than that."

"He didn't smile, did he?"

"No. But he's wearing a red tie."

He had always worn dark ones, fixed to some kind of celluloid collar.

"What does that mean?"

The Baron knew everything, and he would tell everybody's secrets with a thin-lipped smile.

"His wife's away on holiday."

"I thought she was a cripple."

"She was."

"She's cured?"

For years poor Lognon had been obliged, between his spells of duty, to do the marketing and cooking, clean the apartment on Place Constantin-Pecqueur, and as well as all that, to nurse his wife, who had decided to be a permanent invalid.

"She got to know a new tenant who came to live in the house, a woman who talked to her about Pougues-les-Eaux and put it into her head to go and take the cure there. Strange as it may seem, she's gone, without her husband, who can't leave Paris just now, but with the neighbor in question. They're the same age and the neighbor's a widow. . . ."

The comings and goings between offices were getting more and more numerous. Nearly all the members of Maigret's squad had left. Janvier had come back. Lucas was bustling to and fro, his forehead gleaming with sweat. Lapointe appeared from time to time; so did Torrence, Mauvoisin—a new member of the Force—and others. The reporters tried to catch them in passing, but not a word could be got out of them.

Young Mademoiselle Maguy, a reporter for one of the morning papers, arrived before long, looking as cool as though it had not been 90° in the shade all day.

"What have you come here for?"

"The same thing as you."

"Meaning?"

"To wait."

"How did you find out that something was happening?"

She shrugged and applied lipstick.

"How many of them are there in there?" she inquired, pointing at Maigret's door.

"Five or six. You can't count 'em. They go in and out as though they were taking turns."

"Turning on the heat?"

"Well, the fellow must be beginning to feel warm."

"Any beer come up?"

"Yes."

That was a sign. When Maigret sent for a tray of

beer it meant he expected to be there for some time.

"Lognon still with them?"

"Yes."

"Pleased with himself?"

"It's hard to tell, with him. He's wearing a red tie."

"Why?"

"His wife's away for a cure."

She knew what that meant. They belonged to the same crowd.

"Did you see him?"

"Who?"

"The man they're grilling."

"All of him except his face. He was hiding behind his hat."

"Young?"

"Neither young nor old. Over thirty, as far as one could judge."

"How was he dressed?"

"Like anyone else. What color was his suit, Rougin?"

"Dark gray."

"I'd have said beige."

"What did he look like?"

"Anyone you might pass in the street."

Steps were heard on the stairs, and Maguy murmured, as the others looked around, "That must be my photographer."

By half past seven there were five press representatives in the corridor, and they watched the waiter from the Brasserie Dauphine coming upstairs with more beer and some sandwiches.

This time it was big stuff. One by one the reporters went to a little office at the far end of the corridor to telephone to their respective newspapers.

"Shall we go and have some dinner?"

"Suppose he comes out while we're away?"

"But suppose this goes on all night?"

"Shall we send for sandwiches too?"

"Good idea!"

"And some beer?"

The sun was sinking behind the rooftops, but it was still daylight, and though the air was no longer sizzling the heat was just as oppressive.

At half past eight Maigret opened his door. He looked exhausted; his hair was sticking to his forehead. He glanced down the corridor, seemed about to go over to the journalists, but changed his mind, and the door closed again behind him.

"Looks as if things are humming!"

"I told you we were in for a night of it. Were you there when they interrogated Mestorino?"

"I was still in the cradle."

"Twenty-seven hours."

"In August?"

"I don't remember what month it was, but . . ."

Little Maguy's printed cotton dress was clinging to her body; there were big dark circles under the arms, and one could see the outline of her bra and panties through the material.

"What about a game of cards?"

The lamps along the ceiling lit up. Darkness fell. The

office boy on the night shift took up his position at the far end of the corridor.

"Couldn't you let a little air in somehow?"

He went and opened the door and window of an office, then of another office, and after a few moments, by paying great attention, they managed to make out something like a faint breeze.

"That's all I can do for you, gentlemen."

At last, at eleven o'clock, there were sounds of movement from Maigret's office. Lucas came out first and then motioned out the unknown man, who was still holding his hat in front of his face. Lognon brought up the rear. All three walked toward the stairs connecting the Criminal Police with the Law Courts and thence with the cells.

The photographers jostled one another. Rapid flashes lit up the corridor. Less than a minute later the glass door closed again and everyone rushed into Maigret's office, which looked like a battlefield. Glasses, cigarette ends, ash, and torn paper were lying about, and the air smelled of tobacco that was already cold. Maigret himself, still in his shirt sleeves, was standing within the door of his closet, washing his hands in the enamel basin.

"You'll give us a few tips, Superintendent?"

He looked at them with the round eyes he always had on such occasions, not seeming to recognize anyone.

"Tips?" he repeated.

"Who was it?"

"Who?"

"The man who's just left here."

"Somebody with whom I've been having a fairly long talk."

"A witness?"

"I have nothing to tell you."

"Have you put him under arrest?"

He seemed to come to life a little and apologized good-naturedly.

"Gentlemen, I'm really sorry not to be able to give you an answer, but frankly, I have no announcement to make."

"You expect to make one soon?"

"I don't know."

"Are you going to see the examining magistrate, Coméliau?"

"Not tonight."

"Has this some connection with the killer?"

"Once again, forgive me if I can't tell you anything."

"Are you going home?"

"What time is it?"

"Half past eleven."

"In that case the Brasserie Dauphine will still be open; I'll go there and have a bite."

They watched them go—Maigret, Janvier, and Lapointe. Two or three journalists followed them to the *brasserie*, where they had a drink at the bar while the three men sat at a table in the inner room and gave their order to the waiter; they looked tired and worried.

A few minutes later Lognon joined them, but not Lucas.

The four were talking in low tones, and it was impossible to hear what they were saying, or to read anything from their lips.

"Shall we be off? Want a lift home, Maguy?"

"No—to the office."

Not until the door closed behind them did Maigret stretch himself. A very cheerful, very youthful smile spread over his face.

"There we are!" he sighed.

Janvier said, "I think they fell for it."

"And how!"

"What will they write about?"

"I've no idea, but they'll manage to get something sensational out of it. Especially little Rougin."

Rougin was a newcomer to journalism, young and aggressive.

"Suppose they realize we've fooled them?"

"They mustn't realize."

This was almost a new Lognon they had with them, a Lognon who had had three pints of beer since four o'clock that afternoon and who didn't refuse the brandy the proprietor invited them to take.

"How's your wife, old man?"

"She writes that the cure's doing her good. She's only anxious about me."

They didn't laugh at this, or even grin. Some subjects are sacred. All the same he was relaxed, almost optimistic.

"You played your part very well. I'm most grateful. I hope no one except Alfonsi is in the know, at your station?"

"No one."

It was half past twelve when they parted. There were still people sitting outside the cafés, and more people in the street, enjoying the comparative coolness of the night.

"Are you taking the bus?"

Maigret shook his head. He preferred to walk home, alone; and as he went along his excitement diminished and his face took on a graver expression, a look almost of distress.

Several times he passed solitary women who were walking along close to the house fronts, and they always started, as though at his least gesture they would begin running or cry out for help.

In the last six months, five women who, like these, were on their way home or to visit a woman friend, five women walking along the Paris streets, had been murdered by the same man.

The strange thing was that all five crimes had been committed in a single one of the twenty *arrondissements* of Paris, the 18th, in Montmartre; and not only in the same *arrondissement* but in the same district, the small sector that lay between the four Métro stations Lamarck, Abbesses, Place Blanche, and Place Clichy.

The names of the victims and of the streets where they had been attacked, and the hours of the different murders, had become familiar to all newspaper readers, and for Maigret they were a veritable obsession.

He knew the list by heart and could repeat it without thinking, like some fable learned at school.

February 2nd. Avenue Rachel, quite close to the Place Clichy and just off the brightly lit Boulevard de Clichy: Arlette Dutour, aged 28, prostitute, who lived in a cheap hotel on Rue d'Amsterdam.

Two stabs in the back, one of which had caused almost instantaneous death. Clothes methodically torn, and a few superficial lacerations on the body.

No trace of sexual abuse. Her jewelry had not been taken—it was of little value—but neither had her handbag, which contained a fairly substantial sum of money.

March 3rd. Rue Lepic, a little above the Moulin de la Galette. Eight fifteen in the evening. Joséphine Simmer, born at Mulhouse, midwife, aged 43. She lived on Rue Lamarck and had just delivered a woman at the top of the Butte.

A single stab in the back, right to the heart. Clothes torn and superficial lacerations on the body. Her midwife's bag lay beside her on the pavement.

April 17th. (In view of the similarity of dates between February 2nd and March 3rd they had expected another crime on April 4th, but nothing had happened.) Rue Etex, running alongside the Montmartre cemetery, nearly opposite the Hôpital Bretonneau. Three minutes past nine, again at night. Monique Juteaux, dressmaker, aged 24, living with her mother on Boulevard des Batignolles. She had been to see a friend who lived on Avenue de Saint-Ouen. It was raining and she had an umbrella.

Stabbed three times. Lacerations. Nothing stolen.

June 15th. Between twenty past and half past nine. Rue Durantin this time, still in the same sector. Marie Bernard, widow, aged 52, Post Office clerk, living with her daughter and son-in-law in an apartment on Boulevard Rochechouart.

Stabbed twice. Lacerations. The second blow had severed her carotid artery. Nothing stolen.

July 21st. The most recent of the crimes. Georgette Lecoin, a married woman with two children, aged 31, who lived on Rue Lepic, not far from the scene of the second murder.

Her husband was a night worker in a garage. One of her children was ill. She was going down Rue Tholozé, looking for an open pharmacy, and had been killed at about nine forty-five, nearly opposite a dance hall.

Stabbed once. Lacerations.

It was horrible and monotonous. They had sent extra police to the Grandes-Carrières district. Lognon and his colleagues had postponed their vacations. Would they ever be able to take them?

The streets were patrolled. Policemen were stationed at all the strategic points. They had been there already when the second, third, fourth, and fifth murders were committed.

"Tired?" asked Madame Maigret, opening the door of the apartment at the very moment when her husband arrived on the landing.

"It's been a hot day."

"Still nothing?"

"Nothing."

"I heard on the radio just now that there'd been a great commotion at the Quai des Orfèvres."

"Already?"

"It's thought to have some connection with the crimes in the 18th. Is that true?"

"More or less."

"You've picked up a scent?"

"I just don't know."

"Have you had dinner?"

"Yes, and even supper, half an hour ago."

She said no more about it, and before long they were both asleep, with the window wide open.

He got to his office at nine the next morning without having had time to read the newspapers. They were lying on his desk, and he was about to glance through them when the telephone rang. At the first syllable he recognized the voice.

"Maigret?"

"Yes, sir."

It was Coméliau, of course, the examining magistrate in charge of the five Montmartre crimes.

"Is all this true?"

"To what are you referring?"

"To what this morning's papers say."

"I haven't seen them yet."

"You've made an arrest?"

"Not that I know of."

"It would perhaps be best if you came around to my office at once."

"Very well, sir."

Lucas had come in and had been listening to the conversation. He understood the grimace with which the Superintendent said:

"Tell the Chief I've gone to the Law Courts and don't expect to be back in time for the report."

He took the route that had been followed the night before by Lognon, Lucas, and the mysterious visitor to the Criminal Police, the man who held his hat in front of his face. In the examining magistrates' corridor the gendarmes saluted him; some of the accused persons and witnesses who were waiting there recognized him, and a few of them made a slight gesture of greeting.

"Come in. Read that."

He had been expecting all this, naturally, expecting to find Coméliau irritable and aggressive, controlling with difficulty the indignation that made his little mustache quiver.

One of the papers said:

KILLER CAUGHT AT LAST?

Another was headed:

COMMOTION AT THE QUAI DES ORFÈVRES
IS THIS THE MONTMARTRE MANIAC?

"I would like to point out, Superintendent, that yesterday at four o'clock I was here, in my office, less than two hundred yards from your own office and within reach of a telephone. I was still here at five o'clock, at six o'clock, and I did not leave to fulfill other obligations until ten minutes to seven. Even then I could have been reached, first of all at home, where you have frequently telephoned me before now, and afterward at the house of friends whose address I had made a point of leaving with my valet."

Maigret stood listening without a twitch of the eyelid.

"When an event as important as . . ."

The superintendent raised his head and said quietly, "There has been no event."

Coméliau was too excited to calm down immediately; he hit the papers with the flat of his hand.

"What about this? Are you going to tell me the journalists have made it up?"

"They have been making assumptions."

"In other words, nothing whatsoever took place, and these journalists just imagined that you had an unknown man brought to your office, questioned him for more than six hours, and then sent him to the cells, and that . . ."

"I didn't question anybody, sir."

This time Coméliau was shaken; he stared at Maigret with a baffled expression.

"You would do well to explain matters, so that I, in

my turn, may be able to explain them to the Public Prosecutor, whose first idea this morning was to call me up."

"Someone did, it's true, come to see me yesterday afternoon, accompanied by two inspectors."

"Someone these inspectors had arrested?"

"It was more in the nature of a friendly visit."

"Is that why the man hid his face with his hat?"

Coméliau pointed to a photograph spread across two columns on the front page of the various newspapers.

"That may have been just an accident, an automatic gesture. We chatted . . ."

"For six hours?"

"Time passes so quickly."

"And you sent for beer and sandwiches?"

"That's correct, sir."

Coméliau again brought his hand down on the newspaper.

"This gives a detailed account of all your movements."

"I'm sure it does."

"Who was this man?"

"A delightful fellow called Mazet, Pierre Mazet, who worked under me for a time about ten years ago, when he had just passed his examinations. After that, hoping for more rapid promotion—and partly, I think, as a result of some kind of unhappy love affair—he applied for a transfer to Central Africa, where he stayed for five years."

Coméliau, now completely baffled, stood frowning at Maigret, wondering if the superintendent was making fun of him.

"He came down with fever and had to leave Africa, and the doctors won't let him go back. Once he's in good shape again he will probably ask for readmission to the Criminal Police."

"And it was in order to receive him that you cleared the deck for action, as the newspapers don't hesitate to declare?"

Maigret went over to the door and made sure no one was listening outside.

"Yes, sir," he confessed at last. "I needed a man whose description would be as vague as possible and whose face would not be known to the public or to the press. Poor Mazet has changed a great deal while he's been in Africa. You understand?"

"Not very well."

"I made no announcement to the reporters. I didn't utter a single word to suggest that the visit had any connection with the Montmartre crimes."

"But you did not deny it."

"I kept saying I had nothing to say, which was true."

"And the result . . ." the little magistrate exclaimed, again pointing to the newspapers.

"The result I hoped for."

"Without consulting me, of course. Without even keeping me informed."

"Simply in order not to make you share my responsibility, sir."

"What are you hoping for?"

Maigret's pipe had gone out a few minutes before; he relit it with a reflective expression on his face, and then said slowly:

"I don't know yet, sir. I just thought it was worth trying something."

Coméliau was no longer quite sure where he stood, and sat staring at Maigret's pipe, to which he had never become accustomed. The superintendent was the only man who ventured to smoke in this office, and Coméliau regarded it as a form of defiance.

"Sit down," he said at last, reluctantly.

And before sitting down himself, he went and opened the window.

2

Professor Tissot's Theories

It was on the previous Friday that Maigret and his wife had made their tranquil way, in the evening, to a neighborly visit on the Rue Picpus, and all the local streets had been lined with people sitting in their doorways or even on chairs they had taken out to the sidewalk. The traditional monthly dinners with Doctor Pardon still continued, but for the last year or so there had been a slight variation in the system.

Pardon had started inviting some other member of his profession together with the Maigrets; he nearly always chose someone who was interesting either for his own sake or for his line of work; and quite often the superintendent would find himself seated opposite some great specialist or famous surgeon.

He had not realized at first that it was these people who had asked to meet him, and who were studying him as they put endless questions to him. They had all heard about him, and were curious to make his acquaintance. Before long they always found some common ground for discussion, and with the help of an old liqueur the after-dinner conversation in the Pardons' quiet drawing room, where the windows overlooking the busy street were nearly always open, had often continued until quite late at night.

A dozen times the other party to one of these conversations had suddenly looked gravely at Maigret and asked him, "Did you never feel tempted to go in for medicine?"

Maigret, almost shamefaced, would reply that that had been his first intention, but that his father's death had made it necessary for him to give up his studies.

Wasn't it a strange thing that they should feel this, after so many years? Their way of being interested in people, their attitude toward people's troubles and failings, were almost the same as his.

And the policeman did not try to hide the fact that he felt flattered when medical men with world-famous names ended by discussing their work with him just as though he were one of them.

Had Pardon made his choice deliberately that evening because of the Montmartre killer who had been worrying everybody for months? Possibly he had. He was a very simple man, but at the same time he had very delicate and subtle perceptions. He had had to take his vacation early in the season this year, in June, because that was the only time when he could find a substitute.

When Maigret and his wife arrived there were two people already sitting in the drawing room beside the tray of drinks—a broad-shouldered man, built like a peasant, with short, wiry gray hair and a ruddy face, and a dark-complexioned woman of exceptional vivacity.

"My friends the Maigrets . . . Madame Tissot . . . Professor Tissot . . ." said Pardon, making the introductions.

This was the celebrated Tissot, director of Sainte-Anne, the mental hospital on Rue Cabanis. Although he often came into court to give expert evidence, Maigret had never actually met him, and found him to be a solid, human, jovial type of psychiatrist such as he had not come across before.

Before long they sat down to dinner. It was a hot evening, but toward the end of the meal it started to rain, a light gentle rain, and its rustling sound outside the open windows formed an accompaniment to the rest of their talk.

Professor Tissot was not taking a vacation, for though he had an apartment in Paris he went nearly every evening to his country house at Ville-d'Avray.

Like previous guests, while keeping up a random conversation he began scrutinizing the superintendent, with short, rapid glances, each of which seemed to add a touch to the picture of Maigret that he was forming. It was not until they were back in the drawing room, and the women had settled down in a corner of their own accord, that he made a point-blank attack:

"Doesn't your responsibility frighten you a bit?"

Maigret understood at once.

28

"I suppose you're referring to the murders in the 18th *arrondissement?*"

The other man merely blinked. And it was true that for Maigret this was one of the most disturbing cases of his whole career. It wasn't simply a matter of tracking down a criminal. The question, from the standpoint of the community, was not the usual one, of punishing a murderer.

It was a question of defense. Five women were dead, and there was no reason to suppose that things would stop at that.

And the customary methods of defense were not working. This was proved by the fact that the whole police mechanism had been brought into action after the first crime, without preventing the subsequent murders.

Maigret thought he understood what Tissot meant by referring to his responsibility. It was upon him, or, to be more precise, *upon his method of approach to the problem,* that the fate of an unknown number of women would depend.

Had Pardon felt this too, and was that why he had arranged this meeting?

"Although in a way it's my own line," Tissot had gone on, "I wouldn't like to be in your place, with the public getting panic-stricken, the newspapers doing nothing to reassure them, and highly placed people all clamoring for contradictory measures. That's the correct picture, I take it?"

"That's it, all right."

"I imagine you've noted the features of the different crimes?"

He was going straight to the heart of the matter, and Maigret might have been talking to one of his colleagues of the Criminal Police.

"Between ourselves, Superintendent, may I ask what you've found most striking?"

This was a bit of a poser, and Maigret, who seldom found himself in such a situation, felt himself blushing. But he replied without hesitation, "The type of victim. You asked me for the chief feature, didn't you? I'm not talking about the others, of which there are quite a number.

"When there's a series of crimes, as is the case here, the first thing we do at the Quai des Orfèvres is to look for what they have in common."

Tissot nodded approvingly; he was holding a glass of armagnac, and dinner had considerably heightened his color.

"Such as the time?" he inquired.

One could feel he wanted to show that he knew the case, that he too, through the newspapers, had studied it from every angle, including the strictly police angle.

It was Maigret's turn to smile now, for this was rather touching.

"Yes, the time. The first attack took place at eight o'clock in the evening, and it was February. So it was dark by then. The crime on March 3rd was committed a quarter of an hour later, and so on and so forth, the last, in July, having taken place a few minutes before

ten o'clock. Obviously the murderer waits for darkness."

"What about the dates?"

"I've gone over them twenty times, till they ended
by getting mixed up in my mind. On my office desk
you'd see a calendar covered with notes in black, blue,
and red. I've tried every system, every code, as though
I were deciphering a secret language. First of all, people talked about the full moon."

"People always think the moon plays an important
part in actions they can't account for."

"Do you believe it does?"

"As a doctor, no."

"As a man?"

"I don't know."

"In any case, that explanation won't work, because
only two of the five attacks took place on nights when
the moon was full. So I looked for something else. The
day of the week, for example. Some people get drunk
every Saturday. Only one of the crimes was committed
on a Saturday. Then there are occupations where the
weekly holiday doesn't fall on Sunday but on some
other day."

He had the impression that Tissot, too, had considered these different hypotheses.

"The first constant, if I may so call it, that we hit
upon," he continued, "was the district. The murderer
obviously knows that marvelously well, in every nook
and corner. In fact it is thanks to his familiarity with
the streets, the places that are brightly lit and those

that are not, the distance between two given points, that he has not only never been caught, but never been seen."

"The papers have mentioned witnesses who declared they had caught sight of him."

"We've taken statements from them all. The first-floor tenant on the Avenue Rachel, for example, who's the most positive of the lot. She declares he's tall and thin and was wearing a yellowish raincoat and a felt hat pulled down over his eyes. In the first place, that's a standard description which turns up too often in cases like this, and we're always suspicious of it at the Quai. In the second place, it has been proved that from the window where this woman says she was standing, the spot in question can't be seen.

"The evidence of the little boy is more dependable, but too vague to be of any use. That relates to the business on the Rue Durantin. You remember?"

Tissot nodded.

"In short, the man knows the district wonderfully well, and that's why everybody thinks he lives there—which is creating a particularly distressing local atmosphere. They're all looking at their neighbors with suspicion. We've received hundreds of letters describing the strange behavior of perfectly normal people.

"We've considered the hypothesis that the man doesn't live in the district, but works there."

"That's a considerable job."

"It represents thousands of hours. Not to mention the hunting through our files, or the lists of all the criminals and maniacs we've brought up to date and checked. Like all hospitals, yours must have received a questionnaire about the patients you've discharged over the last few years."

"It was answered by my staff."

"The same questionnaire was sent to asylums in the provinces and in foreign countries, and to general practitioners."

"You said something about another constant."

"You'll have seen the photographs of the victims in the newspapers. They were all printed on different dates. I don't know if you've had the curiosity to put them side by side."

Again Tissot nodded.

"The women were all of different origin, geographically to begin with. One was born at Mulhouse, another in the South of France, another in Brittany, and two in Paris or the suburbs.

"From the occupational point of view there was no resemblance between them either: a prostitute, a midwife, a dressmaker, a Post Office clerk, and a housewife.

"They didn't all live in the district.

"We have made certain that they didn't know one another and more than probably had never met."

"I had no idea you made inquiries from so many different angles."

"We went further. We made sure they didn't all attend the same church, for instance, or go to the same butcher, that they didn't have the same doctor or den-

33

tist, that they didn't go, on more or less definite dates, to the same movie house or dance hall. When I say it took thousands of hours . . ."

"With no result?"

"None. In any case, I wasn't expecting results, but I had to check up. We have no right to leave even the smallest possibility unexplored."

"You thought about vacations?"

"I see what you mean. They might have taken their vacations at the same place every year, in the country or by the sea; but they didn't."

"So the murderer chose them at random, as the opportunity occurred?"

Maigret felt sure Professor Tissot didn't believe this, that he had noticed the same thing as he himself had done.

"No. Not altogether. Looking carefully at their photographs one discovers, as I said, that these women did have one point of resemblance—their figures. If you don't look at their faces, only at their figures, you'll notice that all five were shortish and rather plump, almost fat, with thick waists and broad hips, even Monique Juteaux, the youngest of the lot."

Pardon and the Professor exchanged glances, and Pardon's expression said, "I told you so! He'd noticed it too!"

Tissot smiled.

"Congratulations, my dear Superintendent. I see there's nothing I can teach you."

He hesitated for a second, then added:

"I'd mentioned it to Pardon, wondering whether the police would have noticed that point. It was partly for that reason, and partly because I've been wanting to meet you for a long time, that he invited me and my wife this evening."

All this time they had been standing up. At Doctor Pardon's suggestion they now went and sat down in a corner near the window, from where they could hear the sounds of a radio. The rain was still falling, so softly that the tiny drops seemed to be alighting gently one on top of another, to form a kind of dark varnish on the surface of the road.

It was Maigret who resumed the conversation.

"Do you know, Professor, what question it is that worries me the most—the answer to which, if we could find it, would in my opinion lead us to the killer?"

"Go on."

"The man is no longer a child. So he must have lived for quite a number of years—twenty, thirty, or more—without ever committing a crime. Yet in the course of the last six months he has killed five people in succession. The question I'm asking myself is, how did it all begin? Why, on February 2nd, did he suddenly change from a harmless citizen into a dangerous maniac? You're a scientist, do you see any explanation?"

Tissot smiled and threw another glance at his colleague.

"People are very apt to credit us scientists, as you call us, with knowledge and powers we don't possess. But I'll try to answer your question, not only as regards the initial impulse but as regards the case itself.

"I shall not, incidentally, use any scientific or technical terms, for more often than not they merely serve to disguise our ignorance. Isn't that so, Pardon?"

He must be alluding to certain medical men against whom he had a grudge, for Pardon seemed to understand what he meant.

"Confronted with a series of crimes such as we are considering, everybody's first reaction is to declare that a maniac or a lunatic must be responsible for them. By and large, that is correct. To kill five women in the circumstances in which those five murders were committed, for no apparent reason, and then to tear their clothes, is conduct that has nothing in common with that of a sane man, as we understand the term.

"As for why and how it all began, that is a very complicated question, and hard to answer.

"Nearly every week I am called into court to give evidence as an expert. In the course of my career I have seen the concept of the criminal's responsibility changing so rapidly that in my opinion all our ideas about justice have been altered by it, if not actually unsettled.

"In the old days we used to be asked: 'At the time he committed the crime, was the accused responsible for his actions?'

"And the word 'responsibility' had a fairly precise meaning.

"Nowadays we are asked to assess the responsibility of Man, with a capital M; so much so that I often have the impression that the fate of a criminal is no longer determined by the judge and jury, but by us, the psychiatrists.

"Yet in most cases we know no more about it than the layman.

"Psychiatry is a science as long as there is a traumatism, a tumor—that is, an abnormal development in a particular gland or function.

"In such cases, it's true, we can say with a clear conscience whether a man is healthy or sick, whether he is or is not responsible for his actions.

"But those are the rarest cases, and such people are for the most part in an asylum."

"Why do others, probably including the man we are discussing, behave differently from their fellow creatures?"

"In my opinion, Superintendent, you know as much about that as we do, if not more."

Madame Pardon had come over to them with the bottle of armagnac.

"Keep it up, gentlemen. On our side of the room we're exchanging cooking recipes. A little armagnac, Professor?"

"Just half a glass."

They had gone on chatting like this, in a light as soft as the rain that was falling outside, until past one o'clock. Maigret didn't recall the whole of their long conversation, which had often moved over to related subjects.

He remembered that Tissot had said, for example, in

the ironical tone of a man with an old score to settle:

"If I were a blind believer in the theories of Freud, Adler, or even of the present-day psychoanalysts, I wouldn't hesitate to declare that our man has sexual obsessions, although none of the victims was attacked sexually.

"I might also talk about complexes and work back to early childhood impressions. . . ."

"You rule out that explanation?"

"I don't rule out any explanation, but I distrust the ones that are too easy."

"You have no theory of your own?"

"Not a theory, no. An idea, perhaps, but I admit I'm rather afraid to mention it to you, for I'm not forgetting that the responsibility for the investigation rests on your shoulders. It's true that your shoulders are as broad as mine. Son of a peasant, eh?"

"In the Allier."

"I'm from Cantal. My father's eighty-eight and still living on his farm."

One felt he was prouder of this than of his own scientific accomplishments.

"A lot of lunatics, or semilunatics—to use an unscientific term—have passed through my hands after they have committed crimes, and in the matter of constants, as you said a while back, there is one I've found in nearly all of them: a conscious or unconscious need to assert themselves. You understand what I mean by that?"

Maigret nodded.

"Nearly all of them, rightly or wrongly, had for a long time been regarded in their own circle as unstable, second-rate, or mentally retarded, and as a result had felt humiliated. By what process does such humiliation, suppressed for a long time, suddenly break out in the form of a crime, an attack, some gesture of defiance or bravado? Neither I nor, as far as I know, any of my fellow doctors can say for certain.

"What I'm saying is perhaps not orthodox, especially when compressed into a few words, but I am convinced that the majority of crimes which are said to have no motive, and repeated crimes in particular, are a manifestation of wounded pride."

Maigret had become thoughtful.

"That fits in with something I'd noticed," he muttered.

"What's that?"

"That if criminals didn't sooner or later feel the need to boast of what they'd done, there wouldn't be nearly so many of them in prison. Do you know where we go first of all to look for a man who's committed what's known as a sex crime? In the old days we went to the brothels; now that they've ceased to exist we look for him in the arms of some kind of prostitute. And they talk, those men! They feel confident that with such women it doesn't matter, that they run no risk; and in most cases that's true. They tell their whole story. Often they embroider on it."

"You've tried this time?"

"There isn't a tart in Paris, especially in the Clichy

and Montmartre district, who hasn't been questioned in the last few months."

"With no result?"

"None."

"Then that makes it worse."

"You mean that since he hasn't relieved his mind, he's bound to do it again?"

"Virtually bound to."

Maigret had recently been studying all the historic cases that bore some resemblance to the business in the 18th *arrondissement*, from Jack the Ripper to the Düsseldorf Vampire, by way of the Viennese lamplighter and the Pole who operated among the farms in the Aisne Department.

"You think they never stop of their own accord?" he asked. "But there's the precedent of Jack the Ripper, who was never heard of again from one day to the next."

"How do we know he wasn't killed in an accident, or that he didn't die of illness? I'll go further than that, Superintendent, and now I'm not speaking as the medical director of Sainte-Anne, because this takes me too far away from the official theories.

"People like your man are driven, without knowing it, by a need to get themselves caught, and that, again, is a form of vanity. They can't bear the idea that those around them are still taking them for ordinary people. They have to be able to proclaim from the housetops what they've done, what they have been capable of doing.

"I don't mean to say they give themselves away on purpose; but nearly always, as one crime follows another, they take fewer precautions, as though they were defying the police, defying fate.

"Some of them have admitted to me that it came as a relief to them when they were arrested at last."

"I've been told the same thing."

"You see!"

Whose idea had it been? The evening had gone on so long, they had considered and reconsidered the subject from so many angles, that afterward it was difficult to be certain what had come from one of them and what from the other.

Perhaps the suggestion had been put forward by Professor Tissot, but so tactfully that even Pardon had not noticed.

It had been past midnight already when Maigret muttered, as though to himself:

"Suppose someone else were arrested and took the place of our killer, usurping, as it were, what he regards as his fame. . . ."

They had got there now.

"Yes," replied Tissot, "I think your man would have a feeling of frustration."

"It remains to be seen how he would react. And *when* he would react."

Maigret was already ahead of the others, leaving theory behind and considering practical possibilities.

They knew nothing about the killer. They had no description of him. Up to now he had operated in only one district, in one particular sector, but there was no guarantee that he would not break out tomorrow in some other part of Paris or elsewhere.

What made the threat so disturbing was that it remained vague, indefinite.

Would a month go by before his next crime? Or only three days?

All the streets of Paris could not be kept indefinitely in a state of siege. Even the women, who scuttled to their homes after every murder, would soon resume a more normal life, venturing out in the evening, telling themselves the danger was past.

"I have known two cases," Maigret began again after a silence, "of criminals' writing to the newspapers to protest because innocent people had been arrested."

"People like that often write to the papers, driven by what I call their exhibitionism."

"That would help us."

Even a letter composed of words cut out of a newspaper might be a starting point, in an investigation where there was nothing to take hold of.

"Of course he would be faced with another solution. . . ."

"I'd just thought of that."

An extremely simple solution: immediately after the arrest of an alleged criminal, the real one might commit another murder, similar to the previous ones! Perhaps two, or three. . . .

They said good-by outside the house, standing beside the Professor's car. He and his wife were going back to Ville-d'Avray.

"Can we give you a lift home?"

"We live near here, and we're used to walking."

"I have an idea this case will have me back in the criminal courts as an expert."

"Provided I lay hands on the criminal."

"I trust you to do that!"

They shook hands, and Maigret had the impression that this was the beginning of a friendship.

"You didn't have a chance to talk to her," said Madame Maigret a little later, as they were walking along together on their way home. "A pity, because she's the most intelligent woman I've ever met. What's her husband like?"

"A very nice fellow."

She pretended not to notice what Maigret was doing, furtively, as when he was a small boy. The rain was so cool and refreshing that from time to time he would put out his tongue and catch a few drops; they had a taste of their own.

"You seemed to be having a serious discussion."

"Yes. . . ."

That was all they said on the subject. They got back to their house and up to their apartment, where the windows had been left open; the rain had come in a little, and Madame Maigret mopped the floor.

It may have been in his sleep, or it may have been when he woke up next morning, that Maigret reached his decision. And as luck would have it, Pierre Mazet, his ex-inspector whom he hadn't seen for eight years, came to his office that very morning.

"What are you doing in Paris?"

"Nothing, Chief. I'm getting myself fit again. The mosquitoes in Africa didn't do me any good, and the doctors insist that I must rest for a few more months. After that, I'm wondering whether there'd still be a place for me at the Quai."

"I should certainly think so!"

Why not Mazet? He was intelligent, and there was little danger of his being recognized.

"Like to do me a favor?"

"Do you need to ask me, of all people?"

"Come and pick me up about half past twelve, and we'll have lunch together."

Not at the Brasserie Dauphine, they'd certainly be noticed there.

"Or rather, don't come back here, and don't go around the other offices now. Meet me at the Châtelet Métro station instead."

They lunched at a restaurant on Rue Saint-Antoine, and the superintendent explained to Mazet what he wanted him to do.

It would be better, more convincing, if he were not brought to Criminal Police Headquarters by a man belonging to the Quai des Orfèvres, but by inspectors from the 18th *arrondissement;* and Maigret thought at once of Lognon. Who could tell? It might give the man a chance. Instead of patrolling the streets of

44

Montmartre he would be more closely involved in the investigation.

"Choose one of your colleagues who'll keep his mouth shut."

Lognon had chosen Alfonsi.

And the comedy had been acted—with complete success as far as the press was concerned, for all the papers were already talking about a sensational arrest.

Maigret told Coméliau, the examining magistrate, once more:

"They watched certain comings and goings, and drew their own conclusions. Neither I nor my staff told them anything. On the contrary, we denied their suggestions."

It was unusual to see Coméliau smile, even sardonically.

"And suppose that, tonight or tomorrow, because this arrest—or this false arrest—has caused people to neglect their precautions, another crime is committed?"

"I've thought of that. In the first place, for the next few evenings every available man from our own staff and from the station in the 18th *arrondissement* will keep a close watch on the district."

"That has been done already, without result, if I'm not mistaken?"

That was true. But was nothing new to be attempted?

"I've taken another precaution. I went to see the Prefect of Police."

"Without telling me?"

"As I said before, I wish to take the sole responsibility for whatever may happen. I'm only a policeman. You are a magistrate."

The word pleased Coméliau, who struck a more dignified attitude.

"What did you ask the Prefect?"

"For permission to use a certain number of volunteers from the women's section of the municipal police."

This was an auxiliary corps, whose members usually dealt only with matters concerning children and prostitutes.

"He sent for a number of them who satisfied certain conditions."

"Such as?"

"Height and plump figure. From among the volunteers, I selected those with the closest physical resemblance to the five victims. Like them, they will be unassumingly dressed. They will appear to be local women, going about their business, and some of them will carry parcels or baskets."

"In fact you're setting a trap."

"All those I selected have taken physical-training courses and learned judo."

Coméliau was rather nervous all the same.

"Am I to tell the Public Prosecutor about this?"

"Better not."

"You know, Superintendent, I don't like this at all."

To which Maigret replied, with disarming candor, "No more do I, sir!"

46

Which was true. But surely they must try anything that might put an end to the slaughter?

"Officially I know nothing about it, do I?" said Coméliau as he walked to the door with his visitor.

"You know absolutely nothing."

And Maigret wished this were true.

3

A District in a State of Siege

The Baron, who as a reporter had been frequenting
Criminal Police Headquarters for almost as many years
as Maigret, little Rougin, still a youngster but already
knowing the ropes better than most journalists, and
four or five others of less eminence—including Maguy,
who was the most dangerous because for all her air of
innocence she never hesitated to open any door one
had not taken the precaution of locking, or to pick up a
stray paper—together with one or two photographers,
more of them for a time, spent the greater part of the
day in the corridor at the Quai des Orfèvres, where
they had established their main base.

Sometimes most of them went off to the Brasserie
Dauphine in search of refreshments, or to make a telephone call, but they always left somebody behind, so
that the door of Maigret's office was continually under
observation.

Rougin had had the additional idea of sending a
man from his paper to follow Lognon, who found him-

self being trailed from the moment he left his apartment on the Place Constantin-Pecqueur in the morning.

These people knew the racket, as they put it; they were almost as experienced in police business as an inspector with years of seniority.

Yet not one of them suspected what was going on almost before their eyes, the kind of gigantic deployment of forces which had begun in the early hours of the morning, long before Maigret's visit to Coméliau.

For example, inspectors from distant *arrondissements* such as the 12th, 14th, and 15th had left home wearing clothes that were not their usual ones, some of them taking a suitcase or even a trunk; and, acting on instructions, they had been careful to begin by making their way to one of the railway stations.

The heat was almost as oppressive as the day before, and life was proceeding in slow motion except in the districts popular with tourists. Buses full of foreigners were to be seen all over the place, with the voices of guides proceeding from them.

In the 18th, particularly in the sector where the five crimes had been committed, taxis were stopping outside hotels and lodginghouses and people were getting out, with luggage that indicated they had come from the provinces, and asking for rooms; most of them insisted on overlooking the street.

All this was in accordance with a careful plan, and some of the inspectors had been told to bring their wives with them.

It wasn't often that such precautions had to be taken. But this time, could they trust anybody at all? They knew nothing about the killer. This was another aspect of the question which had been discussed by Maigret and Professor Tissot that evening at the Pardons'.

"In fact, in between these impulses he must necessarily behave like an ordinary man, otherwise his peculiarities would already have attracted attention."

"Necessarily, as you say," the psychiatrist had agreed. "Indeed, it's probable that in appearance, behavior, and occupation he's the being whom one would least suspect."

He was not one of the sex-obsessed characters who were known to the police, for ever since February 2nd they had been kept under surveillance, with no result. Nor was he one of those human wrecks or disturbing creatures who attract attention in the streets.

What had he done until his first crime? And what was he doing between one crime and the next?

Was he a man who lived alone in an apartment or in a furnished room?

Maigret would have sworn he wasn't, that he was a married man leading a well-ordered life; and Tissot was inclined to think the same.

"Anything's possible," he had said with a sigh. "If I were told it was one of my own colleagues I wouldn't protest. It may be anybody—a workman, a clerk, a small shopkeeper, or a prominent businessman."

He might also be the manager of one of the hotels

the inspectors were invading, and that was why they couldn't go in in the usual way and say:

"Police. Give me a room overlooking the street, and don't say a word to a soul."

It was safer not to rely on the concierges, either. Nor on the informers who lived in the district.

When Maigret returned to his office after leaving Coméliau, he was assailed by the journalists, just as he had been the evening before.

"You've been in conference with the examining magistrate?"

"I have been to see him, as I do every morning."

"Did you tell him about yesterday's interrogation?"

"We had a chat."

"You still won't say anything?"

"I have nothing to say."

He went to see the Director. The report had been finished some time ago. The big boss, too, was worried.

"Coméliau didn't insist on your giving it up?"

"No. Of course if there's any hitch he'll drop me."

"You still feel confident?"

"I have to."

Maigret was not embarking on this experiment lightheartedly, and he realized what a responsibility he was shouldering.

"Do you think the reporters will go on swallowing it?"

"I'm doing my best to make sure they will."

He was usually on friendly working terms with the press, which can be very helpful at times. But now he

51

must not risk an unintentional give-away. Even the inspectors who were pouring into the Grandes-Carrières district did not yet know exactly what was being planned. They had been ordered to do so-and-so, go to such-and-such a place, and wait for instructions. Naturally, they suspected this had something to do with the killer, but they knew nothing of the operation as a whole.

"Do you think he's a clever man?" Maigret had asked Professor Tissot the other evening.

He had his own idea about that, but hoped for confirmation of it.

"Clever in the same way as most people of that kind. For example, he must instinctively be an excellent actor. Supposing he's a married man, for instance, he has to be able to resume his usual manner, not to mention recovering his self-control, when he arrives home after one of his crimes. Even if he's a bachelor he must meet other people, if only his landlady, his concierge, his cleaning woman, and so on. Next morning he goes to his office or workshop, and people will inevitably talk to him about the Montmartre killer. Yet in six months nobody has suspected him.

"What's more, in six months he has never made a mistake about time or place. No reliable witness claims to have seen him in action, or even running away from the scene of one of his crimes."

This had led Maigret to ask about something that was worrying him.

"I'd like to have your opinion about a particular

point. You just said that he behaves most of the time like an ordinary man; and that presumably means that he thinks more or less like an ordinary man as well?"

"I understand. Very likely."

"Five times he has had what I may call a crisis, five times he has departed from his ordinariness and killed somebody. When does the impulse occur? Do you see what I mean? At what moment does he stop behaving like you or me and begin to behave like a killer? Does it come over him just at any time during the day, and does he wait for darkness while thinking out his course of action? Or does the impulse only come when the opportunity arises—at the moment when he's going along some deserted street and catches sight of a possible victim?"

The reply to this question was of the utmost importance to him, for it might either restrict or extend the field of investigation.

If the impulse came at the moment of the murder, the man must necessarily live in or near the Grandes-Carrières district, or at any rate be obliged to go there in the evening, either because of his work or for some other commonplace reason.

Conversely, the man might come from anywhere, and have chosen the streets leading from the Place Clichy to the Rue Lamarck and the Rue des Abbesses for reasons of convenience or for some reason personal to himself.

Tissot had thought for quite a time before answering.

"I can't, of course, make a diagnosis as though I had the patient in front of me. . . ."

He had said "patient" as though referring to one of his people at Sainte-Anne; this did not escape the superintendent, and it pleased him. It confirmed his impression that they both looked at the tragedy in the same light.

"But in my opinion, if I may make the comparison, there comes a moment when he sets out on the hunt, like a wild animal, a lion or tiger, or simply like a cat. You've watched cats?"

"Often, when I was a boy."

"His movements are no longer the same. He's ready to spring and all his senses are on the alert. He becomes capable of perceiving the faintest sound, the most imperceptible movement, the slightest smell, from a considerable distance. From that time on, he senses dangers and avoids them."

"I see."

"It's rather as though, when he's in that state, our man had second sight."

"I suppose you have no grounds for a hypothesis as to what starts up the mechanism?"

"None. It might be a random memory, the sight of a woman passing in the crowd, a whiff of a particular scent, or a few words overheard. It might be no matter what, such as the sight of a knife, or of a dress of a particular color. Has any attention been paid to the color of the victims' clothes? The papers haven't mentioned that."

"The colors were different, but almost all so neutral that they wouldn't have shown in the dark."

When he got back to his office he took off his jacket and tie, as he had done the day before, unbuttoned his collar, and, because the sun was shining straight onto his chair, lowered the pale-colored blind. After which he opened the door of the inspectors' office.

"You there, Janvier?"

"Yes, Chief."

"Nothing new? No anonymous letters?"

"Only letters from people denouncing their neighbors."

"Get those checked. And have Mazet brought to me."

Mazet had not slept in the jail; he had left the Law Courts by a side door and gone home. But he must have been back in the cells since eight o'clock that morning.

"Shall I go down myself?"

"That would be best."

"Still no handcuffs?"

"No."

He didn't want to cheat to that extent in his game with the journalists. Let them draw whatever conclusions they chose from what they saw. Maigret wouldn't go so far as to load the dice.

"Hello. Give me the Grandes-Carrières police station, please . . . Inspector Lognon . . . Hello—Lognon? . . . Nothing new at your end?"

"Someone was waiting for me outside my door this

55

morning, and followed me. He's across the street from here now."

"Is he concealing himself?"

"No. I think he's a journalist."

"Have his papers checked. Everything going according to plan?"

"I've found three rooms, with friends. They don't know what it's about. Do you want the addresses?"

"No. Come here in about forty-five minutes."

The previous day's scene in the corridor was repeated when Pierre Mazet made his appearance, flanked by two inspectors and with his hat in front of his face again. The photographers got to work. The journalists called out questions that remained unanswered. Maguy managed to knock down the hat, and while she was picking it up from the floor the unknown man hid his face with both hands.

The door was shut again, and Maigret's office promptly took on the aspect of a control room.

The deployment was silently continuing, up the hill, in the quiet streets of Montmartre, where many shops were closed for a fortnight or a month because of the holidays.

More than four hundred people had a part to play— not only those who were watching from the hotels and the few apartments that could be made use of with no danger of giving away the secret, but others who were taking up prearranged positions in the Métro stations, at the bus stops, and in even the most insignificant of the cafés and restaurants that stayed open in the evening.

So that it should not have the air of an invasion, the plan was carried out in stages.

The women police, too, were given detailed instructions by telephone; and Maigret's office was like an army headquarters, with maps spread out on which every individual's position was marked.

Twenty inspectors, from among those not usually seen in public, had hired—not only in Paris, but in the suburbs and as far afield as Versailles—cars with noncommittal registration numbers, which would be parked at the right moment at strategic points, where they would not be noticed among the other cars.

"Send for some beer, Lucas."

"And sandwiches?"

"Yes, just as well."

Not only because of the journalists, to make them think another interrogation was going on, but because everyone was busy and there would be no time to go out for lunch.

Lognon arrived in due course, still wearing his red tie and his straw hat. At first glance one wondered what was different about him, and it was surprising to see how the color of a tie can change a man's appearance. He looked almost gay.

"Did your fellow follow you?"

"Yes. He's in the corridor. He's a reporter, no doubt about it."

"Any of them stay around the station?"

"There's one right inside."

The next newspaper came out about noon. It repeated what had been said in the morning papers, adding that the excitement characteristic of great occasions still prevailed at the Quai des Orfèvres, but that the deepest secrecy was being maintained about the arrested man.

If the police had been able, it said, among other things, *they would no doubt have provided their prisoner with an iron mask.*

That amused Mazet. He was helping the others, making telephone calls himself, marking red and blue crosses on the street plan, delighted to be back in the atmosphere of the building where he felt at home already.

The atmosphere changed when the waiter from the Brasserie Dauphine knocked on the door, for they had to play-act even for him. Once he had gone they flung themselves on the beer and sandwiches.

The afternoon papers published no message from the murderer, who did not seem to intend to communicate with the press.

"I'm going to take a short rest, boys. I'll need to be alert this evening."

Maigret went through the inspectors' office to a small, unoccupied room, where he sat down in an armchair; a few minutes later he was dozing.

About three o'clock he sent Mazet back to the cells and told Janvier and Lucas to take turns having a rest.

Lapointe, wearing blue overalls, was steering a delivery tricycle around the streets of the Grandes-Carrières district. With his cap over one ear and a cigarette stuck to his lower lip, he looked about eighteen years old. From time to time he stopped at some bistro for a white-wine-and-Vichy, and telephoned from there to headquarters.

As time went by everybody began to get restless, and even Maigret lost a little of his confident manner.

There was nothing to show that anything would happen that night. Even if the man decided to assert himself by committing another murder it might not happen until the following evening, or the one after that, or in a week or ten days, and it would not be possible to keep such a large force on the alert for very long.

Nor would it be possible for a secret shared by so many people to be kept for a whole week.

And if the man decided to act right away?

Maigret's conversation with Professor Tissot was always at the back of his mind, and snatches of it were constantly coming to memory.

At what moment would the impulse seize the man? Just now, while the trap was being prepared, he was appearing to all those around him as just an ordinary person. People were talking to him, serving him a meal, no doubt, shaking him by the hand. He was talking too, smiling, perhaps laughing.

Had the spark already been struck? Had it happened this morning, when he saw the papers?

Wouldn't he be rather inclined to say to himself that since the police thought they had caught the criminal they would drop the search, and so he was safe?

What proof was there that Tissot and the superintendent had not been mistaken, that they had not been wrong in their estimate of how the "patient," as the Professor had called him, would react?

Until now he had never killed anyone before evening, he had waited for darkness. But at this very hour, because of the holidays and the heat, there were plenty of streets in Paris where several minutes might go by without a soul being seen.

Maigret remembered the streets in the South of France in the summertime, at the hour of the siesta—their closed shutters, the way in which a whole village or town would sink into torpor every day beneath the torrid sun.

On this very day there were streets in Montmartre which were almost the same.

Moreover, the police had reconstructed the crimes.

At each point where one of them had been committed, the lie of the land was such that the murderer had been able to vanish in the briefest imaginable time. The time would be shorter at night than during the day, of course. But even in broad daylight, given favorable circumstances, he would be able to kill his victim, slash her clothes, and get away in less than two minutes.

Besides, why should it necessarily happen in the street? What would prevent him from knocking at the door of an apartment where he knew he would find a woman alone, and then behaving as he did in the streets? Nothing, except that maniacs—like most criminals, and even thieves—*nearly always* use the same technique and repeat themselves down to the smallest detail.

It would be light until about nine o'clock; it wouldn't be really dark until about half past nine. The moon, now in its third quarter, would not be too bright, and there was a chance that, as on the previous night, it would be veiled by haze.

All these details had their importance.

"Are they still in the corridor?"

"Only the Baron."

They sometimes arranged among themselves for one to keep watch and let the others know if anything happened.

"At six o'clock everyone will leave here as usual, except for Lucas, who will stay on and be joined by Torrence about eight."

Maigret left with Janvier, Lognon, and Mauvoisin, and they all went to the Brasserie Dauphine for a drink.

He got home at seven and had dinner, with the window open onto Boulevard Richard-Lenoir, which was quieter than at any other time of year.

"You've been hot!" remarked Madame Maigret, looking at his shirt. "If you're going out you'd better change."

"I am going out."

"He hasn't confessed?"

He preferred not to answer, for he didn't like lying to her.

"Will you be back late?"

"More than likely."

"Do you still think there's a chance that we can take a vacation once this case is over?"

During the winter they had talked of going to Brittany, to Beuzec-Conq, near Concarneau; but as happened nearly every year, his vacation was postponed from month to month.

"Perhaps," sighed Maigret.

If not, it would mean his plan had miscarried, that the killer had found a loophole in the net, or hadn't reacted as Tissot and he had anticipated. It would also mean fresh victims, impatience among the public and in the press, sarcasm or rage from Coméliau, and even, perhaps, as happened only too often, questions in the Chamber and a demand for explanations from high places.

Worst of all, it would mean the deaths of women, of small, plump women with the look of good housewives who had been out on an errand or visiting friends in the evening in their neighborhood.

"You look tired."

He was not in a hurry to leave. Dinner over, he pottered about the apartment, smoking his pipe, hesitantly pouring himself a small glass of sloe gin, sometimes halting in front of the window where he finally sat down with his elbows propped on the sill.

Madame Maigret did not disturb him. Only when he looked around for his jacket she brought him a clean shirt and helped him put it on. He tried to do it as discreetly as possible, but nevertheless she saw him open a drawer, take out his revolver, and slip it into his pocket.

He didn't often do that. He had no desire to kill anyone, not even a creature as dangerous as this one. All the same, he had ordered all his men to be armed and to protect the women *at all costs*.

He did not go back to the Quai. It was nine o'clock when he got to the corner of the Boulevard Voltaire, where a car—not a police car—was waiting for him with a man at the wheel. The man, who belonged to the police station in the 18th *arrondissement*, wore a chauffeur's uniform.

"Do we start, Chief?"

Maigret, already half concealed by the dusk, got into the back of the car, which now looked like one of those that tourists hire by the day from a garage near the Madeleine or the Opéra.

"Place Clichy?"

"Yes."

On the way he didn't say a word, merely muttering, when they reached the Place Clichy, "Drive up Rue Caulaincourt, not too quickly, as though you were trying to read the numbers of the houses."

The streets in the neighborhood of the boulevards were fairly lively, with people at many of the windows, enjoying the cool of the evening. There were people in various stages of dishevelment on the terraces of all the cafés, down to the very smallest, and at most of the restaurants people were eating out of doors.

It seemed impossible for a crime to be committed in such circumstances; and yet the circumstances had been almost identical when Georgette Lecoin, the most recent of the victims, was killed on the Rue Tholozé, less than fifty yards from a dance hall whose red neon sign lit up the sidewalk.

Anyone who really knew the district could think of a hundred deserted alleys close to the wide, busy streets, a hundred corners where a crime could be committed with practically no risk.

Two minutes. They had calculated that the killer would need only two minutes, and if he were quick enough he might need even less.

What was it that impelled him, his crime once committed, to slash his victim's clothing?

He didn't touch her. He never attempted to uncover her sex, as had been done in certain other cases. He tore the material with great knife slashes, seized by a kind of fury, like a child tearing a doll to pieces or stamping on a toy.

Tissot had spoken of this too, but guardedly. One could feel he was tempted to adopt some of the theories of Freud and his disciples, but it seemed as if he thought that would be too easy.

"One would need to know his past, right back to his childhood, to discover the first shock, which he may not remember himself. . . ."

Every time he thought about the murderer like this, Maigret fell into a fever of impatience. He was in a hurry to be able to conjure up a face, with definite features, a human figure instead of the sort of vague entity that some people called the killer, or the lunatic, or the monster, and that Tissot, involuntarily, as though by a slip of the tongue, had referred to as the patient.

His own helplessness enraged him. This thing was like a challenge flung at him personally.

He would have liked to find himself face to face with the man, no matter where, to look him full in the face, straight in the eye, and to command:

"Now, start talking. . . ."

He had to know. The suspense was harrowing him, preventing him from devoting his full attention to practical details.

Mechanically, he checked the presence of his men at the different points where he had posted them. He didn't know them all personally. Many of them were not on his own staff. But he knew that the figure glimpsed through the curtain of a particular window went by such-and-such a name, and that a certain woman walking past, out of breath, going heaven knew where and moving jerkily because of her absurdly high heels, was one of the police auxiliaries.

Since February, since his first crime, the man had been later on each occasion, ranging from eight in the evening to nine forty-five. But now the days were drawing in instead of getting longer, now that darkness was falling earlier . . . ?

At any moment they might hear a cry from some passer-by who had stumbled in the darkness over a body lying on the sidewalk. That was how most of the victims had been found, nearly always within a few minutes—only once, according to the official pathologist, after about a quarter of an hour.

The car had crossed the Rue Lamarck and entered a sector where nothing had happened up to now.

"What shall I do, Chief?"

"Keep on going, and come back by the Rue des Abbesses."

He could have kept in touch with some of his assistants if he had taken a radio car, but that would have been too conspicuous.

Who could say whether, before each crime, the man didn't spend hours watching the local traffic?

One nearly always knows that a murderer belongs to such-and-such a category; even if one hasn't got a description of him, one has some idea of his general appearance and of the class he comes from.

"Don't let there be a victim tonight!"

It was a prayer like those he used to say as a child, before going to sleep. He wasn't even conscious of uttering it.

"Did you notice?"

"What?"

"The drunkard, by the gas lamp."

"Who was it?"

"A pal of mine, Dutilleux. He loves dressing up, especially as a drunk."

A quarter to ten, and nothing had happened.

"Stop outside the Brasserie Pigalle."

Maigret ordered a beer on his way through, shut himself up in the telephone booth, and called the Criminal Police. It was Lucas who answered.

"Nothing?"

"Nothing so far. Only a prostitute, complaining that a foreign sailor had roughed her up."

"Is Torrence with you?"

"Yes."

"What about the Baron?"

"He must have gone to bed."

It was past the time at which the last crime had been committed. Did that mean the man was less interested in darkness than in the actual time? Or that the sham arrest had had no effect on him?

Maigret was smiling ironically as he returned to the car, and the irony was addressed to himself. Who could tell? The man he was hunting through the Montmartre streets like this might, at this moment, be on vacation at the seaside in Normandy, or in a country boardinghouse.

Discouragement swept over him, suddenly, from one second to the next, as it were. His own efforts and those of his assistants struck him as futile, almost ridiculous.

What was the basis for all this setup, which had taken so long to arrange? Nothing. Less than nothing. A sort of intuition he had had after a good dinner, while he was chatting with Professor Tissot in a quiet drawing room on the Rue Picpus.

And wouldn't Tissot himself be dismayed if he knew how much the superintendent had made out of their casual conversation?

And suppose the man simply was not impelled by vanity, by the need to assert himself?

Even those words, which he had uttered as though he had made a discovery, rather sickened him now.

He had been thinking too much about it. He had worked too hard at the problem. He was ceasing to believe in it, almost beginning to doubt whether the killer really existed.

"Where do we go now, Chief?"

"Wherever you like."

The astonishment he read in the face the man turned toward him made him conscious of his own discouragement, and he was ashamed. He had no right to lose confidence in front of his assistants.

"Go up to the upper end of Rue Lepic."

They went past the Moulin de la Galette, and he looked at the exact spot on the sidewalk where the body of Joséphine Simmer, the midwife, had been found.

So the facts were there. Five crimes had been committed. And the killer was still at large, perhaps ready to strike again.

That woman, aged about forty, hatless, who was coming down the hill with short steps and leading a poodle on a leash—was she one of the auxiliaries?

There were others in the surrounding streets, risking their lives at this very moment. They were volunteers, but the fact remained that it was he who had given them their jobs. It was up to him to protect them.

Had all possible precautions been taken?

On paper this afternoon, the plan had seemed perfect. Each of the sectors regarded as dangerous was under surveillance. The women volunteers were on their guard. Invisible watchers stood ready to intervene.

But had no corner been forgotten? Might not someone relax his attention, if only for a moment?

His discouragement was giving way to fright, and if it were still possible he would perhaps have ordered the whole thing to be stopped.

Hadn't the experiment gone on long enough? It was ten o'clock. Nothing had happened. Nothing would happen now, and it was better so.

The Place du Tertre looked like a fairground. There were crowds around the little tables where people were drinking vin rosé; music blared from every corner, a man was eating fire and another, amid all the clamor, was patiently playing some tune from 1900 on his violin. Yet less than a hundred yards away the alleys were deserted and the killer could take action with no risk.

"Go down again."

"The same way?"

It would have been better to stick to the usual methods, even if they were slow, even if they had yielded no results in six months.

"Go toward the Place Constantin-Pecqueur."

"By the Avenue Junot?"

"If you like."

A few couples were strolling along the sidewalk, arm in arm, and Maigret noticed another, mouth to mouth and with their eyes shut, in a corner just under a gas lamp.

On the Place Constantin-Pecqueur two cafés were still open, and there was no light in Lognon's window. It was he who knew the district best; he would be prowling around the streets like a hunting dog nosing its way through the undergrowth, and for a moment the superintendent imagined him with the dangling tongue and hot breath of a spaniel.

"What time is it?"

"Ten past ten. Nine minutes past, to be precise."

"Hush . . ."

They strained their ears and had the impression that running footsteps could be heard higher up, toward the Avenue Junot, which they had just left behind them.

Before the footsteps there had been another sound— a whistle blast, perhaps two of them.

"Where is it?"

"I don't know."

It was hard to tell the exact direction of the sounds.

While they were still motionless a small black car, one of the Criminal Police cars, rushed close past them, making for the Avenue Junot at top speed.

"Follow that."

Other cars, parked ones which had seemed empty a

few moments before, had now started up and were all tearing in the same direction: two more whistles shrilled through the air, closer this time, for Maigret's car had already covered five hundred yards.

Men's and women's voices could be heard. Somebody was running along the sidewalk, while another figure came hurtling down the stone steps.

Something had happened at last.

4

The Policewomen's Date

At first there was such a confusion in the badly lit streets that it was impossible to make out what was going on, and it was not until much later, by comparing statements that varied in accuracy, that an over-all view could be gathered.

Maigret, whose driver was rushing at top speed up narrow streets which at night took on the aspect of scenes in a theater, no longer knew exactly where he had got to, except that they were approaching the Place du Tertre; he seemed to hear faint echoes of its bands.

What added to the confusion was that there was movement in both directions. Cars and running figures —most of them police, no doubt—were converging toward a point that seemed to lie somewhere on the Rue Norvins, whereas other figures, a bicycle without a lamp, and two, then three cars, were tearing along in the opposite direction.

"That way!" someone shouted. "I saw him go . . ."

They were chasing a man, perhaps one of those the superintendent had seen. He also thought he recognized the Gloomy Inspector—a small figure who was running very fast and had lost his hat—but he couldn't be certain.

What mattered to him at the moment was to find out whether the killer had succeeded, whether a woman had died; and when at last he saw a group of some ten people on a shadowy sidewalk, his first anxious glance was directed toward the ground.

He didn't get the impression that the people were bending down. He could see them gesticulating, and at the corner of an alley a uniformed policeman, who had sprung from heaven only knew where, was already trying to stop the inquisitive crowd that was pouring down from the Place du Tertre.

Someone emerged from the darkness and came up to him as he got out of the car.

"Is that you, Chief?"

The ray of a flashlight picked out his face, as though everyone mistrusted everyone else.

"She's not hurt."

It took him a moment to recognize the speaker, though the man was one of his own inspectors.

"What happened?"

"I don't know, exactly. The man got away. They're chasing him. I'd be surprised if he escapes, with the whole district in a state of siege."

At last he reached the focal point of the excitement, a woman in a rather light blue dress who reminded him of something. She was still breathing fast, but managed to summon a smile, the tremulous smile of one who had had a narrow escape.

She recognized Maigret.

"I'm sorry I didn't manage to get the better of him," she said. "I still can't think how he slipped through my fingers."

She was not sure which of them had already heard the beginning of her adventure.

"Hello! One of his jacket buttons came off in my hand."

She held it out to the superintendent—a little smooth, dark object with the thread still in it, and what might be a scrap of cloth clinging to it as well.

"He attacked you?"

"As I was going past that alley."

A kind of corridor, in complete darkness and with no gate, led out of the street.

"I was on the alert. When I saw the alley I had a kind of hunch, and I had to make an effort to keep on walking at the same pace."

Maigret thought he recognized her now; at any rate, he recognized the blue shade of her dress. Wasn't she the girl he had seen just now on a corner, leaning against a man, their mouths pressed hard against each other?

"He let me get past the opening, and at that very second I sensed a movement, the air stirring behind me. A hand grabbed at my throat and then, I don't know how, I managed a judo hold."

A rumor of what had happened must have gone around the Place du Tertre, and most of the people were leaving the tables with their red-checked cloths, the Venetian lanterns, and the pitchers of vin rosé and streaming in one direction. The uniformed policeman was being overwhelmed. A van of police was coming up the Rue Caulaincourt. They would try to make the crowd move on.

How many inspectors were hunting the fugitive through the neighboring streets, with their unexpected bends and innumerable corners?

Maigret had the impression that from that point of view at least the game was already lost. Once again the killer had had a stroke of genius—that of operating less than a hundred yards away from a kind of fairground, knowing perfectly well that if the alarm were given the crowd would clutter up the whole place.

As far as he could remember—he didn't pause to look at his plan of battle—it was Mauvoisin who was to be at the head of the sector, so he would be directing operations. Maigret looked around for him but couldn't see him.

The superintendent's presence was of no use. The rest, now, was mostly a matter of luck.

"Get into my car," he said to the girl.

He had recognized her as one of the auxiliaries, and it still vexed him to have seen her in a man's arms a little while before.

"What is your name?"

"Marthe Jusserand."

"You are twenty-two years old?"

"Twenty-five."

She was of much the same build as the killer's five victims, but very muscular.

"To Police Headquarters!" said Maigret to the driver.

It would be better for him to go to the place where all information was bound to arrive than to remain in the middle of what seemed like a confused bustle.

A little farther on he saw Mauvoisin, giving instructions to his men.

"I'm going back to the Quai," he called to him. "Keep me informed."

A radio car arrived now. Two others, which must be cruising in the neighborhood, would soon come up as reinforcements.

"Were you frightened?" he asked his companion, after they came to streets where the atmosphere was normal.

On Place Clichy people were crowding out of a movie house. The cafés and bars were brightly lit, reassuring, with people still sitting on their terraces.

"Not so much at the time, but directly afterward. I thought my legs would give way."

"Did you see him?"

"For a second his face was close to mine, and yet I'm not sure whether I'd know him again. I was a physical-training instructor for three years before taking the police exam. I'm very strong, you know. I've learned judo, like the other girls."

"Did you call out?"

"I can't remember."

They were to learn afterward, from an inspector who had been posted at the window of a lodginghouse not far off, that she had not called for help until her aggressor had run away.

"He was wearing a dark suit. He had light brown hair and looked fairly young."

"What age, would you say?"

"I don't know. I was in too much of a state. I knew perfectly well in my mind what I was to do if I were attacked, but when it happened I forgot everything. I was thinking of the knife he had in his hand."

"You saw it?"

She was silent for a few seconds.

"I wonder now whether I saw it, or if I only thought I saw it because I knew it was there. On the other hand, I'd swear his eyes were blue or gray. He seemed to be in pain. I'd managed to get a grip on his forearm, and I must have been hurting him badly. It was a matter of seconds before he would have to bend over and fall flat on the ground."

"And he managed to free himself?"

"I suppose so. He slipped out of my hands, I'm still wondering how. I caught hold of something—his jacket button—and a second later there I was with the button in my hand, while a dim figure was running away. It all happened very quickly, though to me, of course, it seemed to take a long time."

"Would you like a drink to pick you up?"

77

"I never drink. But I'd be glad to have a cigarette."

"Then please smoke."

"I haven't any cigarettes. A month ago I decided to give up smoking."

Maigret stopped the car at the nearest tobacconist's.

"What kind?"

"American, please."

It must have been the first time the superintendent had ever bought American cigarettes.

At the Quai des Orfèvres, where he had her walk upstairs ahead of him, they found Lucas and Torrence each at a telephone. Maigret looked at them questioningly, and they replied, one after another, with a rueful grimace.

The man had not been caught yet.

"Sit down, Mademoiselle."

"I feel quite all right now. So much for the cigarette. It's going to be hard to go without smoking in the next few days."

Lucas had finished his telephone call, and Maigret gave him the description he had just received himself.

"Pass that on to everyone, including the railway stations."

"What height was he?" he asked the girl.

"No taller than I am."

So the fellow was on the short side.

"Thin?"

"Not fat, at any rate."

"Aged twenty? Thirty? Forty?"

She had said "young," but that word can have very different meanings.

"I should say more like thirty."

"Do you remember any other details?"

"No."

"Was he wearing a tie?"

"I suppose so."

"Did he look like a prowling tramp, like a workman, or like an office worker?"

She was doing her best to help, but her recollections were scrappy.

"It seems to me that in any other circumstances I shouldn't have noticed him in the street. He looked like a gentleman, one might say."

Suddenly she put up her hand, like a girl in the schoolroom—and it was not so very long since she had been a schoolgirl.

"He had a ring on his finger."

"A wedding ring or a signet ring?"

"Wait a minute. . . ."

She shut her eyes and seemed to be getting into the same position as during the struggle.

"First of all, I felt it between my fingers, and then, when I put the judo hold on him, his hand came close to my face. . . . A signet ring would have been thicker. . . . There'd have been a flat place on it. . . . It was certainly a wedding ring. . . ."

"You heard that, Lucas?"

"Yes, Chief."

79

"Hair long or short?"

"Not short. I can see it hanging over one of his ears while his head was bent, nearly parallel to the sidewalk."

"Are you taking all this down?"

"Yes, Chief."

"Come into my office."

He automatically took off his jacket, although the night was fairly cool, at least compared with the daytime.

"Sit down. You're sure you won't have a drink?"

"Sure."

"Before the man attacked you, didn't you meet someone else?"

A flood of crimson rose to her cheeks and ears. In spite of her athlete's muscles she had a very thin, soft skin.

"Yes."

"Tell me all about it."

"If I did wrong it can't be helped. I'm engaged."

"What does your fiancé do?"

"He's in his last year of law school. He means to go into the police force too. . . ."

Not the way Maigret had done, from the bottom, beginning on the beat, but through a series of competitive examinations.

"You saw him tonight?"

"Yes."

"You told him what was going to happen?"

"No. I asked him to spend the evening on the Place du Tertre."

"Were you frightened?"

"No. But I liked to feel he wasn't too far away."

"And you arranged another meeting with him?"

She was ill at ease, shifting from one foot to the other, trying to discover, by little glances, whether Maigret was angry or not.

"I'll tell you the whole truth, Superintendent. So much the worse if I made a mistake. We'd been given instructions, you know, to behave as naturally as possible, like any girl or any woman who happens to be out of doors in the evening. And in the evening one often sees a couple kissing and then separating, each going a different way."

"And that's why you arranged for your fiancé to come?"

"Yes, honestly it was. I'd arranged to meet him at ten o'clock. Something was expected to happen before that. So by ten o'clock I wouldn't be risking anything if I tried another way."

Maigret looked closely at her.

"It didn't occur to you that if the murderer saw you leaving a man's arms and going off by yourself, that would probably bring on a crisis?"

"I don't know. I suppose it was just chance. Did I do wrong?"

He thought it wiser not to reply. This was the old dilemma, discipline versus initiative. Hadn't he himself made some serious deviations from discipline, tonight and in the last few days?

"Take your time. Sit down at my desk. And write down, as though you were at school, exactly what happened this evening, trying to remember the smallest details, even those that don't seem important."

He knew from experience that this often produced results.

"May I use your pen?"

"If you like. When you've finished, call me."

He went back to the office where Lucas and Torrence were still sharing the incoming calls. In a tiny room at the end of the corridor a radio operator was writing down the messages from the radio cars on scraps of paper and sending them along by the office boy.

Up in Montmartre they had gradually got rid of most of the crowd, but, as was to be expected, the reporters, alerted, had hastened to the scene.

They had begun by surrounding three blocks of houses, then four, and then a whole district, as time went by, and the man had had the chance to get farther away.

Hotels and lodginghouses were being searched and their occupants waked up, asked for their identity cards, and made to answer a short interrogation.

There was every prospect that the murderer had already slipped away, probably in the first few minutes, when the whistles were blown, people began running, and the inquisitive crowd came pouring out of the Place du Tertre.

There was one other possibility—that the killer lived in the district, close to the scene of this latest attempt, and had simply gone home.

Maigret was fidgeting absently with the button Marthe Jusserand had given him, an ordinary button, dark gray lightly veined with blue. It bore no distinguishing mark. A strand of thick tailor's thread hung from it, and some tiny scraps of cloth from the suit still clung to the thread.

"Call Moers and tell him to come at once."

"Here, or to the laboratory?"

"Here."

He had learned from experience that an hour lost at a certain point in an inquiry might give the criminal a lead of several weeks.

"Lognon would like to speak to you, Chief."

"Where is he?"

"In a café somewhere in Montmartre."

"Hello—Lognon?"

"Yes, Chief. The chase is still going on. They've surrounded a good part of the district. But I'm practically certain I saw the fellow running down the steps leading out of Place Constantin-Pecqueur, just opposite my house."

"You weren't able to catch up with him?"

"No. I ran as fast as I could, but he's quicker than I am."

"You didn't shoot?"

For that had been the order—to shoot at sight, preferably at the legs, on the one condition that it involved no danger to any passer-by.

"I didn't dare, because there was a drunken old woman asleep on the bottom steps and I might have hit her. Afterward it was too late. He melted into the darkness, almost as though he'd vanished into the wall. I searched all around, yard by yard. All the time I had the impression he wasn't far off, that he was watching every movement I made."

"And that's all?"

"Yes. Some of the other fellows arrived then, and we organized a roundup."

"Without discovering anything?"

"Only that about that time a man came into a bar in the Rue Caulaincourt where some customers were playing cards. He didn't stop at the bar but went straight to the telephone booth. So he must have had some tokens in his pocket. He made a call and went out just as he'd come in, without a word, without even looking at the proprietor or the cardplayers. That's what made them notice him. They hadn't a clue as to what was happening."

"Nothing else?"

"He's fair-haired, youngish, slender, and had no hat."

"His suit?"

"Dark. My idea is that he called somebody who came with a car to pick him up at an agreed spot. We

84

never thought of stopping cars with several people in them."

It would indeed have been the first time in the annals of crime that a maniac of this kind was not acting entirely on his own.

"Thanks, old man."

"I'm staying here. We'll keep at it."

"That's all that can be done now."

It might have been only a coincidence. Anybody might go into a bar to make a telephone call and not want a drink, or have time for one.

It worried Maigret, nevertheless. He was remembering the wedding ring the young policewoman had told him about.

Had the man had the nerve to send for his wife to get him out of the police cordon? If so, what explanation had he given her? First thing in the morning she would see the papers, with the story of what had happened in Montmartre.

"Is Moers coming?"

"Right away, Chief. He was reading in bed. I told him to take a taxi."

Marthe Jusserand brought in her composition, that is to say her report on the events she had been through.

"I haven't bothered about style, of course. I've tried to put everything down, as objectively as possible."

He glanced over the two pages, finding nothing new in them, and only when the girl turned away to pick up her handbag did he notice that her dress was torn at the back. This detail suddenly brought home to him

85

the danger to which he had exposed her and the other women volunteers.

"You can go to bed now. I'll tell them to drive you home."

"There's no need, Superintendent. Jean is sure to be down below, and he has his little Renault."

He stared at her, quizzical and amused.

"But you can't have told him to meet you at the Quai des Orfèvres—you couldn't have known you would be coming here."

"No. But he was one of the first to come running from the Place du Tertre. I saw him among the people watching, with the inspectors. He saw me, too, while I was talking to you and when I got into your car. He'll certainly have guessed that you'd be bringing me here."

Maigret was flabbergasted; he held out his hand and muttered, "Well, my child, I wish you good luck with Jean. And thank you. I'm sorry to have given you such a scare. The press must still be kept in the dark about the trap we'd prepared, of course. We shan't give them your name."

"I'd rather you didn't."

"Good night. . . ."

He escorted her politely to the head of the stairs and returned to his inspectors, shaking his head.

"Strange girl," he grumbled.

Torrence, who did not think much of the younger generation, murmured:

"They're all like that nowadays."

Moers came in a few minutes later, as fresh as though he had had a good night's sleep. He didn't know a thing. The plans for hunting down the killer had not been communicated to the laboratory staff.

"A job, Chief?"

Maigret handed him the button, and Moers made a face.

"Is that all?"

"Yes."

Moers turned it first on one side, then on the other.

"Want me to go upstairs and look at it?"

"I'll go with you."

This was almost out of superstition. The telephone calls were still coming in uninterrupted succession. Maigret's confidence had not returned. And yet every time the phone rang he gave an involuntary start, hoping the miracle had happened. Perhaps if he were not there it would happen at last, and they would come to the laboratory to tell him the killer had been caught!

Moers turned on the lights and began by using a magnifying glass, tweezers, and a number of delicate instruments, before putting the thread and the scraps of cloth under the microscope.

"I suppose you want to know where the garment from which this button was torn off was made?"

"I want to know everything it's possible to find out."

"Well, to begin with, although it's an ordinary-looking button, it's of very good quality. It's not the kind

87

used for mass-produced suits. I don't think it will be difficult to find out tomorrow morning where it was made, for there aren't very many button manufacturers. Nearly all of them have their offices on the Rue des Petits-Champs, side by side with the wholesale textile houses."

"And the thread?"

"The same that practically every tailor must use. The cloth interests me more. As you see, it's basically a quite ordinary gray; but there's a light blue thread woven in that gives it a special character. I'd swear the stuff wasn't made in France, but imported from England. And imports of cloth pass through the hands of a limited number of dealers, of whom I can give you a list."

Moers had all kinds of lists, yearbooks, and catalogues, thanks to which he could quickly discover where any object came from, whether it was a weapon, a pair of shoes, or a handkerchief.

"There! As you see, half of the importers have their offices on the Rue des Petits-Champs too. . . ."

In Paris, happily, wholesale firms are still more or less grouped together in particular districts.

"None of the offices opens before eight o'clock, most of them not till nine."

"I'll have a start made with those that open at eight."

"Is that all for tonight?"

"Unless you can think of anything else that might be done."

"I'll try, on the off chance."

He would no doubt try to find, on the thread or in the scraps of cloth, some kind of revealing dust or other substance. Three years previously one criminal had been identified by traces of sawdust on a handkerchief, and another by a spot of printer's ink.

Maigret suddenly felt tired. The tension of the last few days, the last few hours, had left him, and he felt no energy, no interest in anything, no optimism.

Tomorrow morning he would have to face Coméliau and the journalists, who would pester him with awkward questions. What was he going to say to them? He couldn't tell them the truth. Nor could he tell lies all along the line.

When he got down to Criminal Police Headquarters again, he found his ordeal with the reporters was not to take place tomorrow, but at once. The Baron wasn't there, but there were three others, including young Rougin, his eyes sparkling with excitement.

"May we see you in your office, Superintendent?"

He shrugged his shoulders, admitted them, and stared at the three of them, all grasping their notebooks and with pencils at the ready.

"Has your prisoner escaped?"

They were bound to ask him about that business, which was becoming a distinct embarrassment now that things had begun to move so quickly.

"Nobody's escaped."

"You released him?"

"Nobody has been released."

"But the killer has attacked again tonight, hasn't he?"

"A young woman was attacked in the street, not far from the Place du Tertre, but she got off with a fright."

"She wasn't hurt?"

"No."

"Did her attacker pull a knife on her?"

"She isn't sure."

"Isn't she here any longer?"

They looked around them, suspiciously. They must have been told in Montmartre that the young woman had got into the superintendent's car.

"What's her name?"

"Her name is of no importance."

"You're keeping it a secret?"

"Let's say there is no point in publishing it."

"Why? Is she married? Did she have no business being where she was?"

"That's one explanation."

"The right one?"

"I don't know."

"Don't you think this is all very mystifying?"

"The mystery that worries me most is the identity of the killer."

"You've discovered that?"

"Not yet."

"Are there some new factors thanks to which you hope to discover it?"

"Perhaps."

"Naturally, you won't tell us what they are?"

"Naturally not."

"Did the young woman whose name is such a secret actually see her assailant?"

"Indistinctly, but well enough for me to give you a description of him."

Maigret gave the description, incomplete though it was, but said nothing about the button torn off the man's jacket.

"Vague, isn't it?"

"Yesterday it was even vaguer, since we knew nothing whatsoever about him."

He was in a bad mood, and felt vexed with himself for treating them like this. They were doing their job, just as he was. He knew he was annoying them by his answers, and even more by his silences; but he couldn't manage to be his usual friendly self.

"I'm tired, gentlemen."

"Are you going home?"

"As soon as you give me a chance."

"Is the hunt still going on, up there?"

"Yes."

"Are you going to release the man Inspector Lognon brought to you yesterday, and whom you've questioned twice?"

He had to think of a reply.

"That man was never held in custody. He wasn't a suspect, he was a witness whose identity, for certain reasons, cannot be revealed."

"As a matter of precaution?"

"Perhaps."

"He's still being guarded by the police?"

"Yes."

"Wouldn't it have been possible for him to get to Montmartre this evening?"

"No. Any other questions?"

"When we got here you were in the laboratory."

They knew the building almost as well as he did.

"Up there they work on objects, not on guesses."

He looked at them unblinkingly.

"May we conclude that the man on the Rue Norvins left something behind him, perhaps in the hands of his victim?"

"It would be preferable, in the interests of the investigation, not to draw conclusions from my comings and goings. Gentlemen, I'm worn out, and with your permission I will leave. In twenty-four hours, or in forty-eight, I shall perhaps have something to tell you. For the moment you will have to rest content with the description I've given you."

It was half past one by this time. There were pauses now between the telephone calls in the neighboring office, where he went to say good night to Lucas and Torrence.

"Still nothing?"

He only had to look at them to realize that the question was superfluous. The police would continue to surround the district and to search it alley by alley and house by house, until dawn broke, revealing the trash cans lined up along the sidewalks.

"Good night, boys."

To be on the safe side he had kept the car, and the driver was pacing up and down in the courtyard. To get a glass of cold beer he would have had to go a long way, to Montparnasse or somewhere near the Place Pigalle, and he hadn't the heart for it.

Madame Maigret, in her nightdress, opened the front door before he had time to get the key out of his pocket; he went in, grumpily and with a stubborn face, and made for the sideboard where the bottle of sloe gin was kept. It wasn't that he wanted, it was beer; but as he emptied his glass at a gulp he had a kind of impression that he was getting his revenge.

5

The Cigarette Burn

It might have taken weeks. At the Quai des Orfèvres that morning everybody was exhausted, with a bad taste in the mouth. Some of them, like Maigret, had had three or four hours' sleep. Others, who lived in the suburbs, had not slept at all.

Some of them were still up there, searching the Grandes-Carrières district, guarding the Métro stations, watching the men who came out of the houses.

"Did you sleep well, Superintendent?"

It was young Rougin, full of beans, even more vivacious than usual, who had hailed Maigret in the corridor in his high-pitched, slightly metallic voice. He seemed particularly cheerful this morning, and it was only when he saw the paper the young man worked for that the superintendent understood why. He too had taken a risk. The day before, already, and again during the evening, and finally while the three or four of them had been harrying Maigret at the Quai des Orfèvres, he had suspected the truth.

He had no doubt spent the remainder of the night in questioning various people, particularly hotelkeepers.

In any case, his paper carried a big headline:

KILLER ESCAPES FROM POLICE TRAP

Out in the corridor, Rougin must be waiting for Maigret's reaction.

Our good friend Superintendent Maigret, he had written, *will probably not contradict us if we say that the arrest made the day before yesterday, and deliberately kept a great mystery, was only a feint, intended to lure the Montmartre killer into a trap. . . .*

Rougin had gone even further. In the middle of the night he had waked up a well-known psychiatrist and asked him questions not unlike those the superintendent had put to Professor Tissot.

Was it thought that the murderer would come and hang about the Criminal Police Headquarters to get a glimpse of the man who was being accused in his place? That is possible. But it is more likely that they hoped, by wounding his vanity, to drive him into making a fresh attack, in a district previously occupied by a force of police. . . .

Only Rougin's paper took this line. The other reporters were at a loss.

"Still here, are you?" growled Maigret when he saw Lucas. "Aren't you going to bed?"

"I slept for a bit in a chair, and then went for a swim at the Deligny Baths and shaved in my dressing room."

"Who's on hand?"

"Nearly everyone."

"No news, of course?"

Lucas replied with a slight shrug.

"Get me Janvier, Lapointe, and two or three of the others."

He had drunk nothing all night except one pint of beer and a glass of sloe gin, and yet he had a kind of hangover. The sky was covered this morning, but not with real clouds that would have cooled the air a bit. A grayish veil had gradually spread above the city, a grimy mist was slowly drifting down into the streets, heavy with dust, and with a smell of gasoline that got one by the throat.

Maigret opened his window but shut it again almost at once, for the air outside was more stifling than that in the office.

"Get along to Rue des Petits-Champs, men. Here are some addresses. If you don't find anything there, hunt up some others in the telephone directory. Some of you had better deal with the button and the others with the cloth."

He explained what Moers had told him about the wholesalers and the importers.

"It's possible we'll be lucky this time. Keep me informed."

He was still glum, and it wasn't, as they all supposed, because he had had a setback, because the man they were pursuing had managed to slip through the net.

He had expected that. In point of fact, it was not a setback, because his expectations had been proved correct and because they at last had a clue, a starting point, however insignificant it might seem.

His thoughts were on the killer, who was beginning to take definite shape in his mind, now that at least one person had had a glimpse of him. He thought of him, still young, fair-haired, probably melancholy or embittered. Why was it that Maigret would have wagered, at this moment, that he came of a good family and was accustomed to a comfortable life?

He wore a wedding ring. So he had a wife. He had had a father and a mother. He had been a schoolboy, perhaps a university student.

This morning he was alone against the Paris police force, against the entire population of Paris; and he too, no doubt, had read young Rougin's article in the newspaper.

Had he gone to sleep, once he had escaped the ambush in which he had almost been caught?

Assuming that his crimes brought him appeasement, or even a certain sense of well-being, what effect would an unsuccessful attack produce on him?

Without waiting for Coméliau to call him up, Maigret went to the magistrate's office, where he found him reading the newspapers.

"I warned you, Superintendent. You can't say I was enthusiastic about your scheme, or even that I approved of it."

"My men are following a trail."

"Something serious?"

"They have a piece of material evidence in their hands. It's bound to lead somewhere. It may take weeks, or it may take two hours."

It didn't even take two hours. Lapointe's first visit on Rue des Petits-Champs had been to an office where the walls were covered with buttons of all kinds. *Established 1782*, was the announcement inscribed on the door, beneath the names of the firm's two partners. And the collection on the walls included every kind of button manufactured from the beginning.

After showing his police badge, Lapointe asked:

"Is it possible to find out where this button comes from?"

For him, for Maigret, or for anyone else, it was just a button like any other; but the clerk looked at it carefully and replied without hesitation:

"It comes from Mullerbach's, at Colmar."

"Does Mullerbach's have a Paris office?"

"In this building, two floors up."

For as Lapointe and his companion noticed, the whole building was occupied by button merchants.

There was no Monsieur Mullerbach nowadays; the firm was run by the son of a son-in-law of the last Mullerbach. He received the police officers very courteously in his office, looked the button over carefully, and asked:

"What exactly did you want to know?"

"Did your firm make that button?"

"Yes."

"Have you got a list of the tailors to whom you sold buttons of that kind?"

The manufacturer pressed a bell as he explained:

"As you perhaps know, cloth manufacturers change the colors, and even the weave, of most of their goods every year. Before they put their new lines on sale they send us samples, so that we can make buttons to match. The buttons are sold direct to the tailors. . . ."

A young man who seemed prostrated by the heat came in.

"Monsieur Jeanfils, will you look up the reference for this button and bring me the list of the tailors to whom we sold that kind?"

Monsieur Jeanfils went out noiselessly without having opened his mouth. While he was gone his employer went on to describe the workings of the button business to the two police officers. Less than ten minutes later there was a knock on the glass-paneled door. Jeanfils reappeared, and laid the button and a sheet of typewritten paper on the desk.

It was a list of about forty tailors, four at Lyons, two at Bordeaux, one at Lille, a few in other French towns, and the rest in Paris.

"There you are, gentlemen. And good luck."

They were back again on the street, where the noise and bustle came almost as a shock after the cloistered calm that reigned in the offices upstairs.

"What do we do now?" asked Broncard, Lapointe's

companion. "Shall we get down to it at once? I counted. There are twenty-eight in Paris. If we took a taxi . . ."

"Do you know where Janvier went?"

"Yes. Into that big building, or rather into the offices at the far end of the courtyard."

"Wait for him."

He himself went into a little bar with sawdust on the floor, ordered a white wine and soda, and shut himself into the telephone booth. Maigret was still with Coméliau, and Lapointe got on to him there.

"Forty tailors in all," he explained. "Twenty-eight of them in Paris. Shall I start making the rounds?"

"Just keep four or five names and dictate the rest to Lucas; he'll send men out."

Before he had finished dictating, Janvier, Broncard, and a fourth inspector came into the bistro, where they waited for him at the bar. All three were looking pleased. After a moment Janvier came and half opened the glass door.

"Don't hang up," he said, "I have to talk to him too."

"It's not the chief. It's Lucas."

"Let me have him all the same."

Lack of sleep had made them all slightly feverish, with hot breath and eyes that were tired but bright.

"That you, old man? Tell the chief everything's going well. Yes, this is Janvier. We've hit the bull's-eye. A bit of luck, the fellow's suit being made of English cloth. I'll explain; I know the whole routine by now. To make it short, only about ten tailors, so far, have ordered that cloth. A lot more have been sent books of samples. It's those they show their customers, and when a suit is ordered they send for the length. In other words, there's every hope things will move quickly, unless the suit was actually made in England, which isn't likely."

Outside the bistro they split up, each with two or three names on a scrap of paper, and it was like drawing a lottery. One of the four would probably—perhaps that very morning—get hold of the name they had been trying to find for the last six months.

It was young Lapointe who won the big prize. He had reserved the part of the Left Bank around the Boulevard Saint-Germain for himself; he knew it well because he lived there.

The first tailor, on Boulevard Saint-Michel, had indeed ordered a length of the cloth. He was even able to show the inspector the suit he had made from it, for it hadn't been delivered yet; in fact, it wasn't finished, but with one sleeve in place and the collar not sewn on yet, it was waiting for the customer to come for a fitting.

The second address was that of a little Polish tailor, on the third floor of a house on Rue Vaneau. He had only one workman. Lapointe found him sitting on his table; he wore steel-rimmed spectacles.

"Do you recognize this cloth?"

Janvier had asked for several samples for his colleagues.

"Certainly. Why? Do you want a suit?"

"I want the name of the customer for whom you made one."

"It was some time ago."

"How long?"

"It was last autumn."

"You don't remember the customer?"

"I remember him."

"Who was it?"

"Monsieur Moncin, Marcel Moncin."

"Who is Monsieur Moncin?"

"A very nice gentleman, who has bought his clothes from me for several years."

Lapointe was trembling; he hardly dared to believe his ears. The miracle was happening. The man they had been looking for so long, who had caused so much ink to flow, the man the entire police force had spent so many hours in hunting, had suddenly acquired a name. He was about to have an address, a status, and soon, no doubt, a visible shape.

"Does he live in the district?"

"Not far from here, on Boulevard Saint-Germain, next door to the Solférino Métro station."

"Do you know him well?"

"As I know all my customers. He's a well-bred, charming man."

"Is it long since he came to see you?"

"The last time was last November, for an overcoat, not long after I'd made him this suit."

"Do you have his exact address?"

The little tailor turned the pages of a notebook

where names and addresses were written in pencil, with figures, no doubt the prices of the suits, which he crossed through in red when they were paid for.

"Do you know if he's married?"

"His wife has been here with him several times. She always comes to help him choose."

"Is she young?"

"About thirty, I suppose. She's very distinguished, a real lady."

Lapointe could not stop trembling from head to foot. Panic was creeping over him. So close to the goal, he was afraid of some sudden hitch that would send them right back to the beginning.

"Thank you. I may come to see you again."

Forgetting to ask what Marcel Moncin's profession was, he rushed downstairs and hurried to the Boulevard Saint-Germain, where No. 228 *bis* attracted his fascinated gaze. It was an apartment house just like the others along the Boulevard, with wrought-iron balconies. The door was open, showing a corridor with beige-painted walls, at the far end of which the elevator cage was just visible. The concierge's lodge was on the right.

Lapointe almost ached with longing to go in, ask for Moncin's apartment, go up and deal with the killer by himself; but he knew he mustn't.

A uniformed policeman was on duty just opposite the entrance to the Métro; Lapointe hailed him and disclosed his identity.

"Will you watch that house during the few minutes

it will take me to ring up the Quai des Orfèvres?"

"What do I have to do?"

"Nothing. Or rather, if a man of about thirty, lightly built and fairish, should happen to come out, manage to delay him somehow—ask to see his papers, do whatever you like."

"Who is he?"

"His name's Marcel Moncin."

"What's he done?"

Lapointe preferred not to explain that in all probability the man was the Montmartre killer.

A few moments later he was again in a telephone booth.

"The Quai? Give me Superintendent Maigret at once. Lapointe speaking."

He was actually stammering with excitement.

"That you, Chief? Lapointe. Yes. I've found . . . What? . . . Yes . . . His name and his address . . . I'm just opposite his house. . . ."

It suddenly occurred to him that other suits had been made of the same cloth and that this might not be the right one.

"Janvier hasn't phoned? Yes? What did he say?"

Three of the suits had been found, but the descriptions did not correspond to what Marthe Jusserand had said.

"I'm speaking from the Boulevard Saint-Germain . . . I've put a police officer outside the entrance . . . Yes . . . Yes . . . I'll wait for you . . . just a second while I look for the name of this bistro."

He left the telephone booth and read, back to front, the name written in enamel lettering on the window of the café.

"Café Solférino . . ."

Maigret had told him to stay there without showing himself. Less than fifteen minutes later, as he stood at the bar with another white wine and soda in front of him, he saw some small police cars stopping at different points.

Maigret himself got out of one of them; Lapointe thought he looked even bulkier and heavier than usual.

"It was so easy that I'm afraid to believe it, Chief. . . ."

Was Maigret as nervous as himself? If so, it didn't show. Or rather, for anyone who knew him well, it was revealed by a surly, or stubborn, manner.

"What's that you're drinking?"

"A wine and soda."

Maigret made a face.

"Have you any draught beer?"

"Certainly, Monsieur Maigret."

"You know me?"

"I've seen your picture in the papers quite often. And last year, when you were dealing with what was going on opposite, at the Ministry, you came here several times for a drink."

He swallowed his beer.

"Come along."

Meantime there had been a deployment of forces which, though on a smaller scale than that of the night before, was no less thorough. Two inspectors had gone up to the top floor of the house. There were others on the sidewalk outside, and yet others across the Boulevard and at the corner of the street, not to mention a radio car close by.

It would no doubt prove superfluous. Killers of that type seldom defend themselves, at any rate with weapons.

"Do I come with you?"

Maigret nodded, and both men went into the concierge's lodge. It was a cozy place, with a little sitting room divided from the kitchen by a red velvet curtain. The concierge was a woman of about fifty, placid and amiable.

"Can I help you, gentlemen?"

"Monsieur Moncin, please?"

"The second floor, on the left."

"Do you know if he's at home?"

"Very likely. I haven't seen him go out."

"Is Madame Moncin there too?"

"She got back from shopping about half an hour ago."

Maigret could not help thinking of his conversation with Professor Tissot at Pardon's. The house was quiet and comfortable, and its old-fashioned style, dating from the middle of the nineteenth century, had something reassuring about it. The elevator stood waiting for them, well oiled and with its brass handle shining; but they preferred to walk up. There was a thick, dark red carpet on the stairs.

Most of the mats outside the doors—which were of dark wood—bore one or more initials in red, and all the bell pushes were well polished. No sound came from the apartments, and no smell of cooking drifted out to the stairs.

Beside one of the first-floor doors was the brass plate of a lung specialist.

Beside the left-hand door on the second floor there was a brass plate of the same size, but with more stylized, modern lettering, which read:

MARCEL MONCIN
ARCHITECT—INTERIOR DECORATOR

The two men paused and exchanged glances, and Lapointe had the impression that Maigret was as agitated as himself. It was the superintendent who put out his hand and pressed the electric button. They didn't hear the bell ring; it must be somewhere in the depths of the apartment. After what seemed a long time the door was opened by a white-aproned maid, less than twenty years old, who looked at them in surprise and asked:

"What is it?"

"Is Monsieur Moncin at home?"

She seemed embarrassed, and faltered:

"I don't know."

Then he was.

"If you'll wait a minute I'll go and ask Madame . . ."

She had no need to go. A woman appeared at the far

end of the hall—a woman who was still young and who was wearing a dressing gown she must have slipped on for coolness after getting back from her shopping.

"What is it, Odile?"

"Two gentlemen who want to speak to Monsieur, Madame."

She came forward, wrapping the dressing gown around her, staring at Maigret as though he reminded her of someone.

"You want . . . ?" she asked, trying to understand.

"Is your husband here?"

"You mean . . ."

"Oh, he is."

She reddened slightly.

"Yes. But he's asleep."

"I must ask you to wake him."

She hesitated, and then murmured:

"May I ask who . . . ?"

"Criminal Police."

"You're Superintendent Maigret, aren't you? I thought I recognized you. . . ."

Maigret, who had advanced unobtrusively, was now in the hall.

"Please wake your husband. I suppose he got home late, last night?"

"What do you mean?"

"Does he usually sleep in the morning until after eleven?"

She smiled.

"Often. He likes to work in the evening, sometimes late into the night. He's an intellectual, an artist."

"He didn't go out last night?"

"Not that I know of. If you will wait in the drawing room I'll go and tell him."

She had opened the glass-paneled door of a drawing room done in a modern style, which was unexpected in this old house, but which had nothing aggressive about it; Maigret told himself he wouldn't mind living in a setting like this. Only the paintings on the walls displeased him, he couldn't make head or tail of them.

Lapointe stood looking down toward the front door. It was an unnecessary precaution, however, for by now all the entrances would be closely guarded.

The young woman departed with a rustle of silk; she was away only two or three minutes, but by the time she returned she had tidied her hair.

"He'll be here in a moment. Marcel is curiously shy in one way—I sometimes tease him about it: he hates to be seen when he's just out of bed."

"You have separate rooms?"

This gave her a slight shock, but she replied quite simply:

"So do a lot of married couples, don't they?"

And indeed, wasn't it almost the general rule among people belonging to their kind of circle? It meant nothing. What he was trying to decide was whether she was playing a part, whether she knew something, or whether on the contrary she was really wondering what connection there could be between Superintendent Maigret and her husband.

"Does your husband work here?"

"Yes."

She crossed the room and opened a door leading into a spacious office with two windows overlooking the Boulevard Saint-Germain. One could see drawing boards in there, and rolls of paper, and some curious models made of plywood or wire, which resembled stage scenery.

"He works a lot?"

"Too much for his health. He's never been strong. We should have been in the mountains now, we always go at this time of year; but he's accepted a commission which will prevent us from taking a holiday at all."

He had seldom seen a woman so composed, with such self-control. Surely she ought to have been panic-stricken at seeing Maigret arrive like this, considering that the papers were full of the killer and everyone knew he was in charge of the investigation? But she was simply watching him, as though interested to see such a famous man at close quarters.

"I'll go and see if he isn't ready."

Maigret, sitting in an armchair, slowly filled his pipe and lit it; there was another exchange of glances between him and Lapointe, who could hardly keep still.

When the door through which Madame Moncin had vanished opened again it was not she who came in, but a man who looked so young that one was tempted to think there must be some mistake.

He was wearing pajamas in a light shade of beige which emphasized his fair hair, delicate skin, and bright blue eyes.

"I'm sorry to have kept you waiting, gentlemen. . . ."

A smile which had something fragile and childish about it hovered on his lips.

"My wife woke me up just now, to tell me . . ."

Had his wife no curiosity about the purpose of this visit? She did not seem to be coming back. Perhaps she was listening at the door her husband had closed behind him?

"I've been working very hard just lately on the interior decoration of a huge house one of my friends is building on the Normandy coast . . ."

Taking a lawn handkerchief from his pocket, he wiped his forehead and upper lip, which were beaded with sweat.

"It's even hotter than yesterday, isn't it?"

He looked out of the window and saw that the sky was a purplish color.

"It's no use opening the windows. I hope we shall have a storm."

"I must apologize," Maigret began, "for being obliged to ask you some personal questions. To begin with, I would like to see the suit you were wearing yesterday."

This appeared to take him by surprise, but without alarming him. His eyes widened slightly. His lips curled. He seemed to be thinking: What a weird idea!

Then he turned toward the door, saying:

"Excuse me a moment."

After not more than half a minute, if that, he came back with a well-pressed gray suit over his arm. Maigret inspected it and found inside a pocket the name of the little tailor on the Rue Vaneau.

"You were wearing this yesterday?"

"I was."

"In the evening?"

"Until just after dinner. Then I changed into what I'm wearing now, before starting work. I work mostly at night."

"Did you go out after eight o'clock in the evening?"

"I stayed in my office until about two o'clock, or half past two, which explains why I was still asleep when you arrived. I need a lot of sleep, like all high-strung people."

He seemed anxious for their approval; he still seemed more like a student than a man of over thirty.

From close to, however, his face had a worn look which contrasted with its youthful appearance. His complexion had something sickly or faded about it, which was not unattractive, as sometimes happens with women who are past their first youth.

"Might I ask you to show me your whole wardrobe?"

At this he stiffened slightly, as though on the point of protesting, or refusing.

"If you wish. Come this way. . . ."

If his wife had been listening at the door she had

time to get away, for they saw her at the other end of the hall, talking to the servant in a bright, modern kitchen.

Moncin opened another door, leading to a bedroom decorated in a light snuff color, with an unmade day-bed in the middle. He went over and drew back the curtains, for the room was in semidarkness, and then opened the sliding doors of a closet that filled the whole of one wall.

There were six suits hanging at the right-hand end, all of them immaculately pressed, as though they had never been worn or were fresh from the cleaner's. There were also three overcoats, one a light-weight one, a dinner jacket, and a tail coat.

None of the suits was of the same material as the sample Lapointe had in his pocket.

"Will you give it to me?" the superintendent asked him.

He held it out to Moncin.

"Last autumn your tailor made you a suit of this material. Do you remember it?"

Moncin looked at it.

"I remember."

"What has become of it?"

He seemed to reflect. After a moment he said, "I know. Someone standing on a bus platform burned the lapel with a cigarette."

"You took it to be mended?"

"No. I hate anything, no matter what, that has been

damaged. It's a quirk of mine, but I've always been like that. Even when I was a child I'd throw away a toy that had a scratch on it."

"You threw the suit away? You mean you put it in the trash can?"

"No. I gave it away."

"Yourself?"

"Yes. I took it out with me one evening when I was going for a walk by the Seine, as I do now and then, and I gave it to a tramp."

"Was this long ago?"

"Two or three days."

"Be precise, please."

"The evening before last."

In the left-hand section of the closet there were at least a dozen pairs of shoes, lined up on shelves, while in the middle were drawers full of shirts, shorts, pajamas, and handkerchiefs, all in perfect order.

"Where are the shoes you were wearing last evening?"

He didn't contradict himself, or falter.

"I wasn't wearing shoes, I was wearing the slippers I have on now, since I was in my office."

"Will you call the maid? We can go back to the drawing room."

"Odile!" he called in the direction of the kitchen. "Come here a minute."

The girl must have arrived only recently from her native village; she still had a country freshness about her.

"Superintendent Maigret wants to ask you a few questions. Please answer them."

"Very well, sir."

She was not alarmed either, only flustered at finding herself face to face with a public figure who was talked about in the papers.

"Do you sleep in the apartment?"

"No, sir. I have my room on the sixth floor, like the other servants in the house."

"Was it late when you went up last night?"

"About nine o'clock, as it almost always is—as soon as I'd finished the washing up."

"Where was Monsieur Moncin then?"

"In his office."

"How was he dressed?"

"As he is now."

"You're sure of that?"

"Certain."

"How long is it since you saw his gray suit with the little blue line in it?"

She reflected.

"The fact is, I don't look after Monsieur's clothes. He's very . . . very particular about them."

She had almost said "fussy."

"You mean he presses them himself?"

"Yes."

"And you're not allowed to open the closets?"

"Only to put the linen away when it comes back from the laundry."

"You don't know when he last wore his gray suit with the blue thread in it?"

"It seems to me it was two or three days ago."

"You never heard anything said—when you were waiting at table, for example—about a burn on the lapel?"

She looked at her employer as though asking for guidance, and faltered:

"I don't know . . . No . . . I don't listen to what they say at meals. . . . They're nearly always talking about things I don't understand. . . ."

"You may go now."

Marcel Moncin was waiting, smiling calmly, only with beads of sweat along his upper lip.

"I must ask you to get dressed and come with me to the Quai des Orfèvres. My inspector will go with you to your room."

"And into my bathroom as well?"

"Into your bathroom as well—I'm sorry. Meantime, I will have a chat with your wife. I regret all this, Monsieur Moncin, but I cannot do otherwise."

The architect made a vague gesture, as if to say:

"As you wish."

It was only at the door that he looked around and asked: "May I inquire for what reason . . ."

"No, not now. Presently, in my office."

And Maigret, from the hall door, called to Madame Moncin, who was still in the kitchen:

"Would you mind coming here, Madame?"

6

The Division of the Gray-Blue Suit

"Got the right one this time?" young Rougin had jeered while the superintendent and Lapointe were going along the corridor at the Quai des Orfèvres with their prisoner.

Maigret had merely paused, turned his head slowly, and let his eyes rest on the reporter. The young man had coughed slightly, and even the photographers had slacked off a little in their activity.

"Sit down, Monsieur Moncin. If you are too hot you may take your jacket off."

"Thank you. I always keep it on."

True, it was hard to imagine him untidy. Maigret had taken off his own jacket, and now went into the inspectors' office to give some instructions. He looked rather sunk into himself, his neck drawn down between his shoulders, and his eyes sometimes had a blank gaze.

Back in his own office, he arranged his pipes and

filled two of them with precise movements, after motioning to Lapointe to stay where he was and take down what was said. Certain great pianists take their seat like this, hesitating, altering the height of the stool, touching the piano here and there as though to put it in a good humor.

"Have you been married long, Monsieur Moncin?"

"Twelve years."

"May I ask your age?"

"I am thirty-two. I was married when I was twenty."

There was a longish silence during which the superintendent stared at his hands, spread out flat on the desk in front of him.

"You are an architect?"

Moncin corrected him, "Architect—interior decorator."

"That means, I suppose, that you are an architect who specializes in interior decoration?"

He had noticed a slight flush on Moncin's face.

"Not exactly."

"Would you mind explaining to me?"

"I am not allowed to draw up the plans of a building, because I haven't actually a degree in architecture."

"What degree do you have?"

"I began as a painter."

"At what age?"

"Seventeen."

"You had your high school certificate?"

"No. Ever since I was a kid I had wanted to be an

118

artist. The pictures you saw in our drawing room are by me."

Maigret had been unable at the time to guess what they were supposed to represent, but there was something gloomy and morbid about them that had made him uncomfortable. Neither the lines nor the colors were definite. The dominant color was a purplish red which mingled with strange greens that made one think of light filtering down through water; and the paint seemed to have spread of itself, like a drop of ink on a piece of blotting paper.

"In short, you are not a qualified architect, and if I understand you correctly, anybody can call himself a decorator?"

"I appreciate your amiable way of making things clear. I suppose you are trying to imply that I am a failure?"

He was smiling sourly.

"You're entitled to do so. I have heard it before," he went on.

"You have a great many clients?"

"I prefer having a few clients, who trust me and give me a free hand, rather than a great many, who would demand concessions."

Maigret knocked out his pipe and lit another. Rarely had an interrogation opened on such a muted note.

"You were born in Paris?"

"Yes."

"Whereabouts?"

Moncin hesitated for a second.

"At the corner of the Rue Caulaincourt and the Rue de Maistre."

In other words, in the very heart of the sector where the five crimes and the unsuccessful attack had taken place.

"Did you live there long?"

"Until I was married."

"Are your parents still alive?"

"Only my mother."

"Who lives . . . ?"

"Still in the same house, the one where I was born."

"Are you on good terms with her?"

"My mother and I have always got on well."

"What was your father's occupation, Monsieur Moncin?"

This time, again, there was a pause, whereas Maigret had not noticed one when Moncin's mother was referred to.

"He was a butcher."

"In Montmartre?"

"At the address I have given you."

"He died . . . ?"

"When I was fourteen."

"Did your mother sell the business?"

"She put in a manager for a time, and then sold the shop but kept the house, where she has an apartment on the fourth floor."

There came a gentle knock on the door. Maigret went into the inspectors' office and returned with four men, all resembling Moncin in age, height, and general appearance.

They were clerks at the Prefecture, hastily collected by Torrence.

"Will you get up, Monsieur Moncin, and stand with these gentlemen against the wall?"

There was a few minutes' wait, during which no one spoke, and then another knock on the door.

"Come in!" called the superintendent.

Marthe Jusserand appeared, looked surprised to find so many people in the office, glanced first at Maigret and then at the row of men, and frowned when her eye fell on Moncin.

Everyone held his breath. She had turned pale, for she had suddenly understood, and realized the responsibility that rested on her shoulders. She realized it so clearly that she was visibly on the point of weeping from sheer nerves.

"Take your time," said the superintendent encouragingly.

"That's he, isn't it?" she murmured.

"You should know best, since you're the only person to have seen him."

"I have the impression it's he. I feel convinced it is. And yet . . ."

"And yet?"

"I'd like to see him in profile."

"Turn sideways, Monsieur Moncin."

He obeyed, not a muscle of his face moving.

"I'm practically sure. He wasn't wearing the same clothes. And his eyes didn't have the same expression. . . ."

"This evening, Mademoiselle Jusserand, we shall take both of you to the spot where you saw your assailant, with the same lighting, and perhaps with him in the same clothes."

Inspectors were hastening along the banks of the Seine, going around the Place Maubert, searching all the tramps' haunts in Paris, in a search for the suit with the missing button.

"Do you need me any longer?"

"No, thank you. As for you, Monsieur Moncin, you may sit down again. Cigarette?"

"No, thank you, I don't smoke."

Maigret left him in Lapointe's care, having instructed the latter not to ask him any questions or speak to him at all, and to reply evasively if Moncin asked him anything.

In the inspectors' office the superintendent met Lognon, who had come to ask for instructions.

"Would you put your head into my office and take a look at the fellow who's in there with Lapointe, just in case . . ."

Meanwhile he himself called up Coméliau, the examining magistrate, and paid a short visit to the Director's office to put him in the picture. He got back to find the Gloomy Inspector frowning like a man trying in vain to remember something.

"You know him?"

Lognon had been working at the Grandes-Carrières police station for the last twenty-two years. He lived only five hundred yards from the house where Moncin was born.

"I'm sure I've seen him before. But where? In what circumstances?"

"His father was a butcher on the Rue Caulaincourt. He's dead, but his mother is still living in the same house. Come with me."

They took one of the little police cars, and an inspector drove them up to Montmartre.

"I'm still racking my brains. It's exasperating. I'm certain I know him. I could even swear there had been something between us. . . ."

"Perhaps you've given him a parking ticket?"

"It wasn't that. . . . It'll come back to me."

The butcher's shop was a fairly large one, with three or four assistants and a fat woman at the cash desk.

"Am I to go up with you?"

"Yes."

The elevator was a tight fit. The concierge came hurrying when she saw them get in.

"Who's it for?"

"Madame Moncin."

"Fourth floor."

"I know."

The house was clean and well kept, but it was a cut or two below the one on the Boulevard Saint-Germain. The elevator shaft was narrower, so were the doors on the landings; the stairs were polished or varnished, without a carpet, and in most cases there were visiting cards on the doors instead of brass plates.

The woman who opened the door was much younger than Maigret had expected, very thin, and so nervous that her face kept twitching.

"What do you want?"

"Superintendent Maigret, of the Criminal Police."

"You're sure it's me you want to speak to?"

She was as dark as her son was fair, with small, bright eyes and a few stray hairs on her upper lip.

"Come in. I was just cleaning house."

The apartment was perfectly tidy all the same. The rooms were small. The furniture dated from the time of the owner's marriage.

"Did you see your son last evening?"

This was enough to make her stiffen up.

"What have the police got to do with my son?"

"Please be good enough to answer my question."

"Why should I have seen him?"

"I imagine he comes to see you now and then?"

"Often."

"With his wife?"

"I don't see what that has to do with you."

She did not ask them to sit down, and remained standing herself, as though hoping the conversation would be brief. On the walls there were photographs of Marcel Moncin at all ages, some of them taken in the country, and also some drawings and childish paintings, which he must have done when he was small.

124

"Did your son come here last evening?"

"Who told you so?"

"He did come?"

"No."

"Nor during the night?"

"He's not in the habit of coming to see me at night. Are you or are you not going to explain the meaning of these questions? I warn you I shall answer no more of them. I am in my own home and I can keep quiet if I choose."

"Madame Moncin, I regret to inform you that your son is suspected of having committed five murders in the last few months."

She faced him, ready to scratch his eyes out.

"What did you say?"

"We have good reason to believe that he is the man who has been attacking women on street corners in Montmartre, and who missed the mark last night."

She began to tremble, and he had the impression, for no definite reason, that she was acting. He felt her re-action was not the natural reaction of a mother who wasn't expecting anything of this kind.

"You dare to accuse my Marcel! . . . But if I tell you it's not true, that he's innocent, as innocent as . . ."

She turned to look at the photographs of her son as a child, and then said, clenching her hands:

"Look at him! Take a good look at him, and you won't dare to say such abominable things again. . . ."

"Your son has not been here within the last twenty-four hours, has he?"

"No, no, no!" she repeated vehemently.

"When did you last see him?"

"I don't know."

"You don't remember his visits?"

"No."

"Tell me, Madame Moncin, did he have any serious illness as a child?"

"Nothing more serious than measles and an attack of bronchitis. What are you trying to get me to admit? That he's mad? That he's always been mad?"

"When he got married, was it with your approval?"

"Yes. I was fool enough. It was even I who . . ."

She left the sentence unfinished, as though catching it back in mid-flight.

"It was you who arranged the marriage?"

"What does it matter, now?"

"And now you are no longer on good terms with your daughter-in-law?"

"What's it got to do with you? That concerns my son's private life, which is nobody else's business, do you hear, neither mine nor yours. If that woman . . ."

"If that woman . . . ?"

"Nothing! You've arrested Marcel?"

"He is in my office at the Quai des Orfèvres."

"Handcuffed?"

"No."

"You're going to put him in prison?"

"Possibly. In fact, probably. The girl he attacked last night has recognized him."

126

"She's lying. I want to see him. I want to see her too, and tell her . . ."

It was the fourth or fifth sentence she had cut short like that. Her eyes were dry, though glittering with fever or rage.

"Wait a minute. I'm coming with you."

Maigret and Lognon looked at each other. She had not been asked to come. It was she who was suddenly making the decisions, and she could be heard in the next room, the door of which she had left ajar, changing her dress and taking a hat out of its box.

"If you feel awkward about having me with you, I'll take the Métro."

"I warn you the inspector is going to stay here and search the apartment."

She looked at Lognon's skinny form as though about to take him by the scruff of the neck and push him downstairs.

"He is?"

"Yes, Madame. If you want things to be done according to regulations, I am prepared to sign a search warrant."

She didn't reply but, muttering something they could not make out, walked to the door.

"Come along!" she ordered Maigret, adding to Lognon as she stood on the landing:

"As for you, I've a feeling I've seen you before. If you are unlucky enough to break something, or to untidy my wardrobes . . ."

All the way along in the car, seated beside Maigret, she was talking to herself in an undertone.

"Ah, no, it's not going to be like that! I'll go as high up as need be. . . . I'll see the Minister, I'll see the President of the Republic if necessary. . . . As for the newspapers, they'll just have to print what I tell them, and . . ."

In the corridor of the Criminal Police Headquarters she noticed the photographers, and when they turned their cameras on her she walked straight up to them with the obvious intention of wrenching them away. The men had to beat a retreat.

"This way."

When she suddenly found herself in Maigret's office, where, apart from Lapointe, who appeared to be dozing, there was nobody except her son, she stopped, looked at him with relief, and said—not rushing over to him, but enfolding him in a protective gaze:

"Don't be frightened, Marcel. I'm here."

Moncin had got up, and was looking reproachfully at Maigret.

"What are they doing to you? At least they haven't beaten you up?"

"No, Mama."

"They're mad! I tell you they're mad. But I'm going off to find the best lawyer in Paris. I don't care how much he wants. I'll spend my last penny if necessary. I'll sell the house. I'll go and beg in the streets."

"Hush, Mama, hush."

He was almost afraid to look her in the face, and

seemed to be apologizing to the police for her behavior.

"Yvonne knows you're here?"

She looked around for her daughter-in-law. How could she possibly not be at her husband's side at such a moment?

"She knows, Mama."

"What did she say?"

"If you will sit down, Madame . . ."

"I don't need to sit down. What I want is to have my son back. Come along, Marcel. We'll soon see if they dare to keep you."

"I am sorry to have to tell you we shall."

"So, you're arresting him?"

"At any rate I'm keeping him at the disposal of the law."

"It's the same thing. Have you thought it over properly? Do you realize your responsibilities? I warn you I won't be pushed about, I'm going to move heaven and earth . . ."

"Be good enough to sit down and answer a few questions."

"I'm answering nothing whatsoever!"

This time she stalked over to her son and kissed him on both cheeks.

"Don't be afraid, Marcel. Don't let them intimidate you. Mother's here. I'm taking care of you. You'll soon be hearing from me."

She glared at Maigret and walked to the door with an air of determination. Lapointe had an attitude of one waiting for orders. Maigret motioned to him to let her go, and she could be heard in the corridor, shouting heaven knew what at the journalists.

"Your mother seems to be very fond of you."

"I'm all she has left."

"Was she very much attached to your father?"

He opened his mouth to reply, but thought better of it. The superintendent guessed his meaning.

"What kind of man was your father?"

Moncin still hesitated.

"Your mother was not happy with him?"

At this he brought out, in a voice full of repressed anger:

"He was a butcher."

"Were you ashamed of that?"

"I beg you not to ask me such questions, Superintendent. I know perfectly well what you are getting at, and I may tell you you are mistaken all along the line. You see what a state you've put my mother into."

"She put herself into it."

"I suppose that somewhere or other, on Boulevard Saint-Germain or elsewhere, your men are now putting my wife through the same treatment."

It was Maigret's turn to keep silent.

"There is nothing she can tell you. Any more than my mother. Any more than I can myself. Question me as much as you like, but leave them in peace."

"Sit down."

"Again? Will it be long?"

"Probably."

"I suppose I shall get nothing to eat or drink?"

"What would you like?"

"Some water."

"You wouldn't rather have beer?"

"I don't drink beer, or wine, or spirits."

"And you don't smoke," said Maigret pensively.

He drew Lapointe over to the half-open door.

"Begin questioning him, little by little, without pushing things too far. Talk to him again about that suit; ask him what he was doing on February 2nd and March 3rd—on all the dates when crimes were committed in Montmartre. Try to find out whether he goes to see his mother on any particular day, whether it's during the day or at night, and why she and his wife have quarreled. . . ."

He himself went off to lunch alone at the Brasserie Dauphine, where he had a table to himself and ordered stewed veal because it smelled good, like home cooking.

He called up his wife to tell her he wouldn't be home for lunch, and very nearly called up Professor Tissot as well. He would have liked to see him, to chat with him again the way they had done in the Pardons' drawing room. But Tissot was a busy man, like himself. Besides, Maigret had no specific questions to put to him.

He was tired and depressed, for no definite reason. He felt he was close to the goal. Things had moved faster than he would have dared to hope. Marthe Jusserand's attitude spoke for itself, and if she had not been more positive it was because she had scruples. The story of the suit given to a tramp didn't hold water. In any case they would no doubt soon hear more about that, for there are not so very many tramps in Paris and practically all of them are known to the police.

"You don't need me any longer, Chief?"

This was Mazet, who had taken the role of the supposed criminal, and now had nothing left to do.

"I went around to the Quai. They let me take a look at the fellow. Do you think it's he?"

Maigret shrugged his shoulders. More than anything else, he felt the need to understand. It is easy to understand a man who has robbed his victim, or who has killed someone to escape being caught, or out of jealousy, or in a fit of rage, or even to make sure of an inheritance.

That kind of crime, the common or garden crime, as one might say, sometimes gave him a lot of trouble, but didn't upset him.

"Imbeciles!" he would growl on such occasions.

For, like some of his illustrious predecessors, he maintained that if a criminal were intelligent he would not need to kill anyone.

Nevertheless, he was able to put himself in their place, to reconstruct their arguments or the sequence of their emotions.

Faced with a man like Marcel Moncin, he felt like a tyro; so much so that he hadn't yet dared to push the interrogation to its limit.

This was not just a man like other men, who had broken the laws of society and put himself more or less consciously beyond the pale.

He was a man unlike others, a man who killed without any of the reasons other people can understand, in an almost childish way, afterward tearing his victims' clothing as though by whim.

Yet in a certain sense Moncin was intelligent. There had been nothing particularly abnormal about his early years. He had got married and seemed to be on good terms with his wife. And though his mother was a bit much, there was certainly an affinity between them.

Did he realize he was lost? Had he realized it this morning, when his wife had gone to wake him up and had told him the police were waiting for him in the drawing room?

What were the reactions of a man like that? Was he unhappy? In between his crimes, did he feel shame or hatred of himself and his instincts? Or did it give him a kind of satisfaction to feel that he was different from other people, different in a way he might think of as superior?

"Coffee, Maigret?"

"Yes."

"Brandy?"

No! If he drank he might get drowsy, and he felt heavy enough as it was, as he nearly always did at a certain point of a case, when he was trying to identify himself with the people he had to deal with.

"It seems you've got him?"

He stared at the proprietor, round-eyed.

"It's in the early afternoon papers. They seem to think it's the right man this time. He's certainly given you trouble, that fellow! Some people were saying he'd never be found, like Jack the Ripper."

He drank his coffee, lit a pipe, and went out into the hot, motionless air imprisoned between the paving stones and the lowering sky, which was slowly turning slate color.

Some sort of tramp was sitting, cap in hand, in the inspectors' office, and he was wearing a jacket that did not go with the rest of his outfit.

It was Marcel Moncin's famous jacket.

"Where did you find this fellow?" Maigret asked his men.

"Down by the river, near the Pont d'Austerlitz."

Maigret put his questions not to the tramp, but to his own inspectors.

"What does he say?"

"That he found the jacket on the riverbank."

"When?"

"This morning at six o'clock."

"And the trousers?"

"They were there too. He was with a pal. They divided the suit between them. We haven't laid hands on the one with the trousers yet, but it won't take long."

Maigret went up to the poor devil, bent down, and saw that there was indeed a hole in the lapel, made by a cigarette burn.

"Take that off."

He had no shirt underneath, only a torn undershirt.

"You're sure it was this morning?"

"My friend will tell you the same. He's Big Paul. All these gentlemen know him."

So did Maigret. He handed the garment to Torrence.

"Take it up to Moers. I don't know whether it's possible, but it seems to me they should be able to discover, by testing, whether a burn in cloth is recent or old. Tell him that in the present case it's a question of forty-eight hours. You understand?"

"I understand, Chief."

"If the lapel was burned last night or this morning . . ."

He waved a hand toward his own office.

"Where have they got to, in there?"

"Lapointe has had beer and sandwiches sent up."

"For both of them?"

"The sandwiches, yes. The other fellow drank Vichy water."

Maigret opened the door. Lapointe was sitting in his chair, bending over some papers on which he was making notes, and trying to think of another question to ask.

"You shouldn't have opened the window. It only lets in hot air."

He went and shut it. Moncin's eyes followed him with a reproachful expression, like some defenseless animal being tormented by children.

"Let's see."

He glanced over the notes, questions and answers, which taught him nothing.

"No fresh developments?"

"Maître Rivière telephoned to say he was to be the counsel for the defendant. He wanted to come right away. I asked him to speak to the examining magistrate."

"That's right. And then?"

"Janvier called up from the Boulevard Saint-Germain. In the office there are erasing knives of all sorts, which might have been used for the various crimes. He also found, in the bedroom, a switchblade knife of a well-known type, which has a blade only about three inches long."

Doctor Paul, the official pathologist who had carried out the post-mortems, had had a lot to say about the weapon, which intrigued him. Crimes of this kind are usually committed with a fairly large knife, such as a butcher's knife or a carving knife, or else with a dagger or a stiletto.

"To judge by the shape and depth of the wounds," he had said, "I am tempted to think the criminal used an ordinary penknife. An ordinary penknife would have closed up, of course. This one must at least have had a safety catch. In my opinion the weapon is not dangerous in itself. What makes it fatal is the skill with which it is used."

"We have found your jacket, Monsieur Moncin."

"Down by the river?"

"Yes."

He opened his mouth, but no words came out. What had he been about to ask?

"Have you had enough to eat?"

The tray was still there and there was half a ham sandwich left. The Vichy water bottle was empty.

"Tired?"

He responded with a half-smile of resignation. Everything about him, including his clothes, was in half-tones. He had retained from his boyhood something timid and charming which was hard to define. Did it come from his fair hair, his complexion, his blue eyes, or from delicate health?

By tomorrow he would no doubt be in the hands of doctors and psychiatrists. But one must not go too fast. Afterward it would be too late.

"I'll take your place," Maigret said to Lapointe.

"Can I go?"

"Wait in the other room. Let me know if Moers finds anything new."

When the door was shut again he took off his jacket, dropped into his armchair, and put his elbows on the desk.

For perhaps five minutes he let his gaze weigh on Marcel Moncin, who had turned his head aside and was staring at the window.

"Are you very unhappy?" he said softly at last, as though in spite of himself.

The other man started, avoided his eyes, and paused for a second before replying:

"Why should I be unhappy?"

"When did you discover you were not like other people?"

The man's face quivered, but he managed to say with a derisive titter:

"You find I'm not like other people?"

"When you were a young man . . ."

"Well, what?"

"Did you know already?"

Maigret had a feeling, at that moment, that if he could find exactly the right words the barrier between himself and the man sitting stiffly in his chair on the other side of the desk would be broken down. He had not imagined that quiver. For a few seconds the tension had been reduced, and very little would have been needed, no doubt, to bring tears into Moncin's eyes.

"You realize, do you not, that you are in no danger either of execution or of a prison sentence?"

Had Maigret chosen the wrong tactics—the wrong words?

Moncin had drawn himself up again, recovered his self-control, his appearance of absolute calm.

"I am in no danger of anything, since I am innocent."

"Innocent of what?"

"Of what you are accusing me of. I have nothing more to say to you. I shall answer no more questions."

These were not light words. One could feel he had made a decision and would stick to it.

"As you like," sighed the superintendent, pressing a bell.

7

Trusting in Providence!

Maigret had made a mistake. Would another man, in his situation, have avoided it? That was a question he was often to ask himself afterward, and of course he never found a satisfactory answer to it.

It must have been about half past three when he went up to the laboratory and Moers asked:

"Did you get my note?"

"No."

"I just sent you one; I expect you passed my man on your way up. The burn on the jacket is not more than twelve hours old. If you'd like me to explain . . ."

"No. You're sure of what you're saying?"

"Certain. All the same, I'm going to make some experiments. I suppose there's no reason why I shouldn't burn the jacket in two other places, in the back, for example? Those burns might be useful as controls if the case comes up for trial."

Maigret nodded and went downstairs again. At that moment Marcel Moncin must already have been in the

Criminal Records office, where he would strip for a preliminary medical examination and for the usual measurements to be taken, and then, dressed again but without a tie, be photographed full face and in profile.

The newspapers were already publishing photographs their reporters had taken when he had arrived at the Quai, and several inspectors, likewise armed with photographs, were going over the Grandes-Carrières district yet again, endlessly putting the same questions to the staff of the Métro, to shopkeepers, to anyone who might have noticed Moncin the evening before or on the evening of one of the earlier crimes.

In the courtyard of the Criminal Police Headquarters the superintendent got into one of the waiting cars and had himself driven to the Boulevard Saint-Germain. The maid he had seen in the morning answered the bell.

"The other gentleman's in the drawing room," she informed him.

She meant Janvier, who was there by himself, making clean copies of the notes he had made during his search.

Both men were equally tired.

"Where's his wife?"

"About half an hour ago she asked me if she might go and lie down."

"How did she behave until then?"

"I didn't see much of her. Now and then she came and put her head into whatever room I was in, to see what I was up to."

"You didn't ask her any questions?"

"You didn't tell me to."

"I suppose you haven't found anything interesting?"

"I had a chat with the maid. She's only been here six months. The Moncins entertain very little and seldom go out. They don't seem to have any close friends. From time to time they go for the weekend to her parents, who it seems have a house out at Triel, where they live all the year round."

"What sort of people?"

"The father had a pharmacy on Place Clichy; he retired a few years ago."

Janvier showed Maigret a photograph of a group in a garden. Moncin was there in a light suit, his wife in a thin dress, a man with a pepper-and-salt beard, and a fattish woman who stood smiling broadly, with her hand resting on the hood of a large car.

"And here's another. The young woman with the two children is Madame Moncin's sister, who is married to a garage owner at Levallois. They have a brother too, who lives in Africa."

There was a box full of photographs, chiefly of Madame Moncin, including one in her First Communion dress, and the inevitable portrait of the couple on their wedding day.

"A few business letters, not many. He seems to have only about a dozen clients. Bills. From what I can see, they don't pay them until they've been sent in three or four times."

Madame Moncin, who had perhaps heard the super-intendent arrive, or had been warned by the maid, now appeared in the doorway. Her face looked more strained than in the morning, and she had obviously been tidying her hair and repowdering.

"Haven't you brought him back?" she asked.

"Not until he gives us a satisfactory explanation of certain coincidences."

"You really believe it was he?"

He made no reply, and she did not begin to protest vigorously, but merely shrugged her shoulders.

"One day you will see you were mistaken, and then you'll be sorry for the harm you're doing him."

"You love him?"

The moment he had asked the question it struck him as foolish.

"He's my husband," she replied.

Did that mean she did love him or simply that, as his wife, it was her duty to stand by him?

"You've put him in jail?"

"Not yet. He's at the Quai des Orfèvres. We're going to question him again."

"What does he say?"

"He refuses to answer. You really have nothing to tell me, Madame Moncin?"

"Nothing."

"You realize, don't you, that even if your husband is guilty, as I have every reason to suppose, he will get neither the guillotine nor hard labor? I told him that just now. I have no doubt the doctors will say he is not responsible for his actions. The man who kills five women in the street and then slashes their clothes is a sick man. When he is not in a moment of crisis, he may deceive people. He certainly does, for no one has found his behavior strange until now. Are you listening?"

"I'm listening."

She was listening, perhaps, but one might have supposed that this digression did not concern her and in no way related to her husband. At moments her eyes were even following the movements of a fly as it climbed up a muslin curtain.

"Five women have died so far, and as long as the killer, or the maniac, or the lunatic, call him what you like, remains at liberty, other lives will be in danger. Do you realize that? And do you realize that although up to now he has attacked only women going along the street, the process may change, and perhaps tomorrow he may begin to attack the people around him? Aren't you afraid?"

"No."

"You don't have the impression that for months, perhaps for years, you yourself have been in mortal danger?"

"No."

It was disheartening. Her attitude was not even defiant. She remained calm, almost serene.

"Have you seen my mother-in-law? What did she say?"

"She protested. May I ask why the two of you are on bad terms?"

"I don't care to speak about it. It is of no importance."

What more could he do?

"You can come now, Janvier."

"You're not going to send my husband back to me?"

"No."

She went with them to the door and shut it behind them. That was about all for that afternoon. Maigret had dinner with Lapointe and Janvier, while Lucas took his turn at remaining alone with Marcel Moncin in the superintendent's office. Afterward they had to resort to a stratagem to get the suspect out of the Criminal Police building, because the corridors and waiting rooms were full of journalists and photographers.

A few big drops of rain had splashed onto the sidewalks at about eight o'clock, and everyone had hoped for a thunderstorm; but if there was one at all it must have broken somewhere toward the east, where the sky was still a poisonous-looking black.

They did not wait until the exact time at which the previous evening's unsuccessful attack had taken place, for by nine o'clock the streets were dark as they had been then, and the lighting was precisely the same.

Maigret went out alone, down the main staircase, chatting with the reporters. Lucas and Janvier pretended to take Moncin away to the cells—he was handcuffed now—but once downstairs they went to the

145

central police station and put him into a car there.

They all met at the corner of the Rue Norvins, where Marthe Jusserand was already waiting, accompanied by her fiancé.

It only took a few minutes. Moncin was led to the exact spot where the girl had been attacked. He was wearing the burned jacket again.

"There were no other lights?"

The girl looked around and then shook her head.

"No. It was just the same."

"Now try to look at him from the angle at which you saw him."

She bent in various ways, had the man moved to two or three places.

"You recognize him?"

Very agitated, her breast heaving, she cast a rapid glance at her fiancé, who was standing at a tactful distance, and murmured:

"It's my duty to tell the truth, isn't it?"

"It is your duty."

She looked again at Moncin, as though to ask his pardon; he was waiting with no sign of interest.

"I am certain it was he."

"You formally identify him?"

She nodded and then her courage left her and she burst into tears.

"I shan't need you any more this evening. Thank you very much," said Maigret, pushing her toward her fiancé. "You heard that, Monsieur Moncin?"

"I heard."

"You have nothing to say?"

"Nothing."

"Take him back, you two."

"Good night, Chief."

"Good night, boys."

Maigret got into one of the cars.

"Drive me home, Boulevard Richard-Lenoir."

But this time he stopped the car just off the Square d'Anvers and went into a *brasserie* to have a beer. His own role was almost finished. Tomorrow morning Coméliau would no doubt want to interrogate Moncin, and would then send him to the specialists for a mental examination.

The Criminal Police would be left with the routine work of looking for witnesses, questioning them, and compiling the fullest possible record.

Why Maigret did not feel satisfied was another story. From the professional standpoint he had done all he had to do. Only, he didn't understand, even yet. There had been no "shock." He had never, at any moment, had the impression of a human contact between himself and Moncin.

Madame Moncin's attitude worried him too. He would have another go at her.

"You look done in," remarked Madame Maigret. "Is it really over?"

"Who says so?"

"The papers. And the radio."

He shrugged his shoulders. After all these years she still believed what she read in the papers!

147

"In a certain sense, yes, it's over."

He went into the bedroom and began to undress.

"I hope you'll be able to sleep a bit late tomorrow morning?"

He hoped so too. He was not so much tired as disgusted, though he couldn't have said exactly why.

"Are you cross?"

"No. Don't worry. You know I often get like this in cases of this kind."

With the excitement of the investigation and the search having come to an end, one suddenly found oneself in a kind of vacuum.

"You shouldn't pay any attention. Pour me a small glass of sloe gin, and let me sleep like a log for ten hours."

He didn't look at the time before he fell asleep; he tossed and turned for a while between sheets that were already damp; a dog was howling persistently somewhere not far off.

He had lost all idea of time and of everything else, even of where he was, when the telephone rang. After it had rung for a good bit, he put out his hand, so clumsily that he upset the glass of water that stood on the night table.

"Hello . . ."

His voice was hoarse.

"Is that you, Superintendent?"

"Who's speaking?"

"Lognon here. . . . I'm sorry to disturb you. . . ."

The Gloomy Inspector's voice sounded somehow melancholy.

"Yes. I'm listening. Where are you?"

"On the Rue de Maistre . . ."

And lowering his voice, Lognon went on, as though reluctantly:

"There's just been another crime. . . . A woman . . . Stabbed several times . . . Her dress has been slashed. . . ."

Madame Maigret had put the light on. She watched her husband, who had been lying down until then, sitting up and rubbing his eyes.

"You're sure? . . . Hello—Lognon?"

"Yes. I'm still here."

"When? And to begin with, what time is it?"

"Ten past twelve."

"When did it happen?"

"About three-quarters of an hour ago. I tried to get you at the Quai. I was all alone at my station."

"I'll be right there . . ."

"Another?" his wife asked.

He nodded.

"I thought the murderer was locked up?"

"Moncin is in the cells. Get the Criminal Police on the line for me while I'm dressing."

"Hello . . . Criminal Police? . . . Superintendent Maigret wants to speak to you. . . ."

"Hello—who's that?" Maigret growled. "That you, Mauvoisin? You've already heard, from Lognon? I suppose our man hasn't budged? . . . What? . . . You've just checked up on that? . . . I'm dealing with it . . . Will you send me a car at once? . . . Yes, to my house. . . ."

Madame Maigret realized that the best she could do in the circumstances was to keep quiet, and it was she who opened the sideboard and poured a glass of sloe gin, which she handed to her husband. He drank it mechanically, and she followed him out to the landing and listened as the sound of his footsteps receded down the stairs.

On the way to Montmartre he never opened his mouth, but sat staring ahead of him; and when he got out of the car, close to a group of some twenty people standing at a dimly lit spot on the Rue de Maistre, he banged the car door behind him.

Lognon came to meet him with the face of one announcing a family bereavement.

"I was on night duty when the news came through by telephone. I came here at once."

There was an ambulance standing by the curb, with the attendants waiting for orders; they could be seen as paler forms in the darkness. There were also a few idlers, standing in timid silence.

A female figure lay on the pavement, almost touching the wall, and a trickle of blood zigzagged away from it, dark and already coagulating.

"Dead?"

A man approached Maigret—a local doctor, he learned afterward.

"I counted at least six knife strokes," he said. "I was only able to make a superficial examination."

"In the back, as usual?"

"No. At least four in the chest. Another in the throat, which seems to have been delivered after the others, probably when the victim had already fallen to the ground."

"The *coup de grâce*," laughed Maigret bitterly.

Didn't it mean that for him, too, this crime was a sort of *coup de grâce*?

"There are other wounds, more superficial, on the forearms and hands."

At this Maigret frowned.

"Do we know who she is?" he asked, pointing to the body.

"I found her identity card in her handbag. Jeanine Laurent, a maid working for Monsieur and Madame Durandeau on the Rue de Clignancourt."

"Her age?"

"Nineteen."

Maigret preferred not to look at her. The poor child was wearing what must have been her best dress; it was made of sky-blue tulle, almost a ball dress. She had doubtless been out dancing. She was wearing very high-heeled shoes, one of which had fallen off.

"Who gave the alarm?"

"I did, Superintendent."

The speaker was a cycle patrolman who had been waiting patiently for his turn.

"I was making my round with a fellow officer, here

present, when I noticed, on the left-hand side-walk . . ."

He had seen nothing of what happened. When he found the body it had still been warm and the wounds were still bleeding. Because of that, he had thought for an instant that the girl was not dead.

"Take her to the Forensic Institute and inform Doctor Paul," said Maigret. He added, turning to Lognon:

"Did you give any orders?"

"I've sent all the men I could find to search the district."

What was the use? Hadn't that been done before, to no purpose?

A car drove up at full speed and stopped with a squeal of brakes. Young Rougin got out of it, his hair bristling.

"Well, my dear Superintendent?"

"Who told you?"

Maigret was gruff, aggressive.

"Someone on the street . . . There are still some people who think the press has its uses . . . So it still wasn't the right fellow?"

Withdrawing his attention from the superintendent, he hurried across to the sidewalk, followed by his photographer, who got down to work while Rougin questioned the bystanders.

"You see to the rest of it," Maigret muttered to Lognon.

"You don't need anyone?"

Maigret shook his head and went back to his car, his

eyes on the ground, with the expression of one brooding over unpalatable thoughts.

"Where do we go, Chief?" asked his driver.

He looked at the man, not knowing what to reply.

"Go downhill, any way, toward the Place Clichy or the Place Blanche."

There was nothing for him to do at the Quai des Or-fevres. What was there that hadn't been tried already?

And he hadn't the heart to go back to bed.

"Wait here for me."

They had reached the bright lights of the Place Blanche, where some of the café terraces were still lit up.

"What will you have?"

"Whatever you like."

"Beer? Brandy?"

"A beer."

At a nearby table a woman with platinum-blonde hair, her breasts half emerging from a skin-tight dress, was talking in a low voice to the man she was with, trying to persuade him to take her to a night club the neon sign of which could be seen directly across the street.

"I promise you you won't regret it. It's expensive, perhaps, but . . ."

Did the man understand? He was an American or an Englishman; he kept shaking his head and saying:

"*No! . . . No!*"

"Is that all you know how to say—*No! . . . No! . . .*? And suppose I say *No* too, and leave you? . . ."

He smiled placidly at her, and she called impatiently to the waiter to bring another round of drinks.

"You can give me a sandwich as well, if he won't go across the way and have supper. . . ."

At another table people were discussing the different scenes of a show they had just seen at a neighboring cabaret. An Arab was selling peanuts. An old flower seller recognized Maigret and thought it wiser to take herself off.

He smoked at least three pipes without moving, while he watched the people going by, and the taxis, and listened to snatches of conversation, as though he felt the need to steep himself in an everyday atmosphere again.

A woman of about forty, fat but still appetizing, who was sitting alone at a table with a *menthe à l'eau* in front of her, was sending winning smiles in his direction, with no idea who he was.

Maigret signed to the waiter.

"The same again," he ordered.

He must give himself time to calm down. Just now, on the Rue de Maistre, his first impulse had been to rush back to headquarters, go to Marcel Moncin's cell, and shake him until he decided to talk.

"Admit that it was you, you filthy swine."

He felt a certainty that was almost physically painful. It was not possible that he had been mistaken all along the line. And what he felt now for the sham architect was not pity or even curiosity. It was anger, almost rage.

This evaporated little by little, in the relative cool of the night, as he watched the scene in the street.

He had made a mistake, he knew that; and now he knew what it had been.

It was too late to put things right now, when a young girl was dead, a country girl who, like thousands of others every year, had come to try her luck in Paris, and who had gone dancing after a day spent in the kitchen.

It was too late even to get confirmation of the idea that had occurred to him. By this time he would find nothing. And if any clues did exist, if there were any chance of finding some witnesses, it could wait till morning.

His men were as worn out as he was. The thing had been going on too long. In the morning, when they read their newspapers in the Métro or the bus, on their way to the Quai des Orfèvres, they would all feel the same stupefaction, the same despondency that had descended on the superintendent just now. Might not some of them begin to lose confidence in him?

Lognon had been embarrassed when he called up; and on the Rue de Maistre he had almost seemed to be commiserating with him.

Maigret could imagine Coméliau's reaction, his imperious telephone call the moment he opened his newspaper.

He went inside the *brasserie* with a heavy step and asked at the bar for a telephone token. He wanted to call his wife.

"Is that you?" she exclaimed, in surprise.

"I only wanted to tell you I shan't be back tonight."

For no definite reason. He had nothing to do for the time being, except to stew in his own juice. He felt a need to get back to the familiar atmosphere of the Quai des Orfèvres, to his own office, with a few of his men.

He did not want to sleep. There would be time for that once the thing was really over; then, perhaps, he might even decide to put in for leave.

It was always like that. He promised himself a holiday and then, when the moment arrived, found some excuse to stay in Paris.

"Waiter, the check."

He paid and walked out to the little car.

"To the Quai."

There he found Mauvoisin with two or three of the others, one of whom was eating sausage and washing it down with red wine.

"Don't bother about me, boys. Nothing new come in?"

"Always the same thing. They're questioning the passers-by. They've arrested two foreigners whose papers weren't in order."

"Call Janvier and Lapointe. Ask them both to be here at five thirty this morning."

For about an hour, alone in his office, he read and reread the minutes of the interrogations, paying particular attention to those of Moncin's mother and wife.

After that he slumped back in his chair, unbuttoned

his shirt to the waist, and seemed to doze off, facing the window. Perhaps he did actually fall asleep? He didn't realize it, but in any case he didn't hear Mauvoisin, who came into his office once and withdrew again on tiptoe.

The windowpanes turned from dark to pale, the sky became gray, then blue, and at last the sun broke through. When Mauvoisin came in for the second time he was carrying a cup of coffee; he had just made some on an electric plate. Janvier had arrived, and Lapointe would be there any minute.

"What time is it?"

"Twenty-five past five."

"Are they there?"

"Janvier is. As for Lapointe . . ."

"Here I am, Chief," came the voice of the last-named.

Both of them were freshly shaved, whereas those who had been up all night had bristly cheeks and muddy complexions.

"Come in, both of you."

Was he making another mistake in not getting in touch with the examining magistrate? If so, he would accept full responsibility, as in the other instances.

"Janvier, you get along to the Rue Caulaincourt. Take one of the other fellows with you, it doesn't matter which, whoever's the freshest."

"To the old woman's apartment?"

"Yes. Bring her here to me. She'll protest, she'll most likely refuse to come."

"Sure to."

Maigret held out a paper he had just signed as though trying to break the nib on it.

"Give her this subpoena. And you, Lapointe, go to the Boulevard Saint-Germain and get Madame Moncin."

"Are you giving me a subpoena too?"

"Yes. Though in her case I doubt whether it's absolutely necessary. Then put them both together in an office, lock them up safely, and come and tell me."

"The Baron and Rougin are in the corridor."

"Naturally!"

"It doesn't matter?"

"They can see them."

The two men went together to the inspectors' office, where the lights were still burning, and Maigret opened his cupboard. He always kept his shaving things there. While he was about the business he cut his upper lip slightly.

"Any coffee left, Mauvoisin?" he called out.

"In just a moment, Chief. I'm making a second batch."

Outside, the first tugs had come to life and were off to collect from the riverbanks the strings of barges they were to haul up or down stream. A few buses were crossing the almost deserted Pont Saint-Michel, and just beside the bridge a fisherman had settled down with rod and line, his legs dangling above the dark water.

Maigret began going to and fro, avoiding the corridor and the reporters, while the inspectors were careful not to ask him any questions, or even to meet his eye.

"Lognon didn't call up?"

"Yes, about four o'clock, to say there were no new developments, except that the young girl definitely had been to a dance hall somewhere near the Place du Tertre. She used to go there once a week, she had no steady boyfriend."

"She left by herself?"

"The boys think so, though they're not sure. They have the impression she was a good girl."

Sounds could be heard in the corridor: a woman talking in a high-pitched voice, though the words were indistinguishable.

A few seconds later Janvier came into the office, looking like a man who has just carried out a disagreeable job.

"Done it! It wasn't altogether easy."

"Was she in bed?"

"Yes. To begin with, she talked to me through the door; she wouldn't open it. I had to threaten to fetch a locksmith. In the end she got into a dressing gown."

"You waited while she got dressed?"

"Out on the landing. She still wouldn't let me into the apartment."

"She's by herself now?"

"Yes. Here's the key."

159

"Go and wait for Lapointe in the corridor."

After about ten minutes both inspectors came into Maigret's office.

"They're there?"

"Yes."

"Did the sparks begin to fly?"

"After one glance they pretended not to know each other."

Janvier hesitated and then ventured a question.

"What are we to do now?"

"For the moment, nothing. You go and sit in the next-door office, near the communicating door. If they decide to talk, try to hear what they say."

"And if they don't?"

Maigret made a vague gesture which seemed to say, "We must trust in providence!"

8

Moncin Gets Cross

Nine o'clock came, and the two women, confined in a very small office, had still not uttered a word. Each of them sat motionless on her straight-backed chair—for the room had no easy chairs—as though in some doctor's or dentist's waiting room that did not offer the resource of magazines to look at.

"One of them got up and opened the window," Janvier told Maigret, who had gone in search of news. "Then she went back to her place and I've heard nothing since."

Maigret had overlooked the fact that at least one of them knew nothing of last night's crime.

"Have some newspapers taken in. Have them put on the desk as though that were the usual thing, but making sure that from where they're sitting they can both see the headlines."

Coméliau had already telephoned twice, first from home, where he had read the paper over breakfast, and again from the Law Courts.

"Tell him I'm somewhere about the building and that they've gone to look for me."

One important question had already been cleared up by a couple of inspectors Maigret had sent out early that morning. So far as Moncin's mother was concerned, the answer was plain. She could go in or out of the house on the Rue Caulaincourt at any hour of the night, for she had kept a key from the time when she owned the whole place. And the concierge put her light out and went to bed at ten o'clock, or half past at the latest.

The Moncins had no key to the front door on Boulevard Saint-Germain, and there the concierge went to bed later, about eleven o'clock. Was that why all the crimes, except last night's, had taken place fairly early? As long as she was still up and the front door was open, the concierge paid little attention to any tenants who might be coming back from the movies, from the theater, or from an evening with friends.

In the morning she opened the door at about half past five, dragged the trash cans out onto the sidewalk, and went indoors again to get dressed. Occasionally she went back to bed for an hour.

That explained how Marcel Moncin could have slipped out without being seen, after the unsuccessful attack, so as to get rid of the suit by leaving it on the riverbank.

Could his wife have gone out on the previous evening and got back fairly late, probably after midnight, without the concierge recollecting that she had pulled the cord to open the door for her?

The inspector who had been sent to Boulevard Saint-Germain said yes.

"The concierge denies it, of course," he explained to Maigret. "But the tenants don't agree. Since her husband died she has got into the habit, every evening, of taking two or three little glasses of some kind of liqueur that comes from the Pyrenees. Sometimes they have to ring two or three times before she opens the door, and when she does she's half asleep, and doesn't hear the name they mutter as they go past the lodge."

Other information was coming in pell-mell, some of it by telephone. They learned, for example, that Marcel Moncin and his wife had known each other since childhood, and had gone to the same primary school. One summer, when Marcel was nine years old, the wife of the pharmacist on Boulevard de Clichy had taken him along on holiday with her own children, to a house they had rented at Etretat.

It was also discovered that after their marriage the young couple had lived for several months in an apartment that old Madame Moncin had let them have in the Rue Caulaincourt house, on the same floor as her own.

At half past nine Maigret made up his mind.

"Tell someone to bring Moncin up here from the cells. Unless, of course, he's already in Coméliau's office."

Janvier, from his observation post, had heard one of the two women get up, and then the rustle of a newspaper. He didn't know which of them it had been. No voice had been raised.

The weather was bright again, the sunshine dazzling; but the heat was not so oppressive as on the last few days, for a breeze was stirring the leaves of the trees, and sometimes the papers on Maigret's desk.

Moncin came in without a word, looked at the superintendent with an imperceptible nod of greeting, and waited to be told to sit down. He had had no chance to shave, and his fair beard was softening the firm lines of his face slightly, making it look weaker, the features somehow blurred—from fatigue too, no doubt.

"Have you been informed of what happened last night?"

He answered, as though reproachfully:

"No one has spoken to me at all."

"Read that."

Maigret held out the paper which gave the fullest report on what had happened on the Rue de Maistre. While the prisoner was reading, the superintendent never took his eyes off him, and he felt certain he was not mistaken in thinking that *Moncin's first reaction was annoyance.* He had frowned, as though surprised and displeased.

IN SPITE OF DECORATOR'S ARREST,
ANOTHER VICTIM IN MONTMARTRE

For a second Moncin seemed to think it was a trap, perhaps that a special copy of the newspaper had been printed to make him give himself away. He read with concentration, checked the date at the top of the page, finally recognized that the report was genuine.

Wasn't he feeling a kind of suppressed anger, as though something were being spoiled for him?

At the same time he was reflecting, trying to understand; and finally he seemed to have hit on the solution of the problem.

"As you see," said Maigret, "someone is doing the utmost to save you. So much the worse if it costs the life of a poor girl who's only just come to Paris!"

Didn't Moncin's lips twitch in a furtive smile? He tried to repress it, but all the same it betrayed a childish satisfaction, quickly concealed.

"The two women are here," Maigret went on casually, pretending not to look at the other man.

It was a curious struggle, he didn't remember one like it before. Neither of them was sure of his ground. The slightest shade of expression was important, a glance, a quiver of the lips, a blinking eyelid.

If Moncin was tired, the superintendent was even more so; and he, in addition, was disgusted. He had once again felt tempted to hand the whole thing over, as it stood, to the examining magistrate and leave him to make what he could of it.

"They'll be brought in presently, and you can have it out among yourselves."

What were Moncin's feelings at that moment? Was

he furious? Perhaps. His blue eyes went blank, he clenched his teeth and threw the superintendent a reproachful glance. But he might be frightened, too, for at the same time sweat broke out on his forehead and upper lip, as it had on the previous day.

"You are still determined to keep silent?"

"I have nothing to say."

"Aren't you beginning to feel it's time to finish with all this? Don't you think, Moncin, that this makes at least *one crime* too many? If you had talked yesterday, this one wouldn't have been committed."

"It has nothing to do with me."

"You know, don't you, which of them foolishly made up her mind to save you?"

Moncin was no longer smiling. On the contrary, his face hardened again, as though he were angry with the woman who had done that.

"Well, I'll tell you what I think about you. You are probably a sick man, for I prefer to believe that no man whose brain was normal would do what you have done, in any circumstances. But that is a question for the psychiatrists. So much the worse if they say you are responsible for your actions."

He was watching Moncin closely all the time.

"You'd be vexed, wouldn't you, if they decided you were irresponsible?"

For the man's pale eyes had gleamed for a second.

"Never mind. You were just an ordinary child, at least in appearance. A butcher's son. Did you feel humiliated at being a butcher's son?"

He did not need a reply.

"It made your mother feel humiliated too; she saw you as a kind of aristocrat who had strayed onto the Rue Caulaincourt. I don't know what your father looked like, poor fellow. Among all the photographs your mother has piously preserved, I didn't find one of him. She's ashamed of him, I suppose. Whereas you, from the time you were a baby, were photographed from every angle, and at the age of six you went to a fancy-dress party as an eighteenth-century *marquis*, in an expensive suit that had been made for you. You love your mother, Monsieur Moncin?"

The man still said nothing.

"Didn't you find it irksome, in the long run, to be fussed over like that, treated like a delicate creature in need of continual care?

"You might have rebelled, as so many boys do in such circumstances, you might have broken away. Listen to me. Other people will take you in hand later on, and they may not be too gentle about it.

"For me, you're still a human being. Don't you understand that that's precisely what I'm trying to do—to strike a little human spark out of you?

"You didn't rebel, because you're lazy and your vanity is without bounds.

"Some people are born with a title, with money, with servants and a whole system of comfort and luxury around them.

"You were born with a mother who took the place of all that for you.

"Whatever might happen to you, your mother was there. You knew it. You could do whatever you chose.

"Only you had to pay for it—by submissiveness.

"You belonged to your mother. You were her property. You were not allowed to grow up into an ordinary man.

"Was it she who married you off at the age of twenty, for fear you'd begin to have love affairs?"

Moncin was staring at him intently, but it was impossible to guess what was at the back of his mind. One thing was certain: he was flattered at receiving so much attention, at the idea that an important man like Maigret should be studying his behavior and trying to read his thoughts.

If the superintendent suddenly made a slip, wouldn't he react, protest?

"I don't think you were in love, because you're too self-centered for that. You married Yvonne for the sake of peace, and perhaps in the hope of escaping from your mother's influence.

"When she was still a little girl, Yvonne was lost in admiration for you, such a fair-haired, elegant boy. You seemed to be made of different clay from your little school friends, even if you were a butcher's son.

"Your mother was taken in. She thought Yvonne was just a little goose with whom she could do as she liked; and she set you both up in the apartment across the landing from hers, so that she could keep a firm hold over you.

"But all that put together doesn't explain the killings, does it?

"The real explanation won't come from the doctors, who will only be able, like me, to shed light on one aspect of the problem.

"You're the only one who knows the whole story.

"And I'm convinced that you would never be capable of explaining yourself."

This time he extorted a smile with a touch of defiance in it. Did that mean that, if he chose, Moncin could make his behavior comprehensible to everybody?

"I've nearly finished. The little goose turned out to be not only a real wife, but a female as possessive as your mother. A battle began between the two of them, with you as the stake, while you, no doubt, were dragged in both directions.

"Your wife won the first round, for she got you away from the Rue Caulaincourt and transplanted you to an apartment on Boulevard Saint-Germain.

"She gave you a new outlook, new surroundings, new friends; and from time to time you slipped away and went back to Montmartre.

"Didn't you begin to feel rebellious toward Yvonne, just as you used to toward your mother?

"*Both of them, Moncin, were preventing you from being a man!*"

The prisoner threw him a glance charged with resentment, and then looked down at the carpet.

"That's what you imagined, what you tried hard to

believe. But at the bottom of your heart you knew quite well it wasn't true.

"You hadn't the courage to be a man. You weren't one. You needed them, the atmosphere they created around you, their attention, their admiration, their indulgence.

"And that was precisely what humiliated you."

Maigret went and stood at the window to recover his breath. He took out his handkerchief and mopped his forehead; his nerves were on edge, like those of an actor at the climax of his role.

"You won't answer—all right, and I know why you can't bring yourself to answer: it would be too painful for your vanity. You suffer too acutely from your own cowardice, from the perpetual compromise in which your life has been passed.

"How many times have you wanted to kill them? I don't mean the poor unknown girls you've been attacking in the street. I mean your mother and your wife.

"I'd bet that when you were still a kid, or in your teens, the idea of gaining your freedom by killing your mother sometimes passed through your mind.

"Not as a real plan, no! Just one of those stray thoughts one forgets immediately, or ascribes to a moment of rage.

"And it was the same later, with Yvonne.

"You were the prisoner of them both. They fed you, looked after you, spoiled you, but at the same time they owned you. You were their creature, their property, something they fought over.

"And you, tossed to and fro between Rue Caulain-court and Boulevard Saint-Germain, you went about like a ghost, so as to get peace.

"When, why, under the stress of what emotion, of what humiliation, worse than the others, was the thing triggered? I have no idea. Only you could answer that question, and I'm not even sure that you could.

"Anyhow, a plan for asserting yourself came into your mind, vaguely at first, then more and more definitely.

"How could you assert yourself?

"Not in your profession, for you know you have always been a failure, or what's worse, an amateur. No one takes you seriously.

"So how are you to assert yourself? By what outstanding action?

"To satisfy your vanity it would have to be outstanding, it must be something everybody would talk about, something that would make you feel far superior to the common herd.

"Did you then have the idea of killing the two women?

"That would be dangerous. The search would automatically lead in your direction, and there would be no one left to back you up, flatter you, encourage you.

"But it was they, the domineering females, that you resented.

"And it was females you turned upon, in the street, haphazardly.

"Did it come as a relief, Moncin, to discover that you

were capable of killing someone? Did it give you the impression that you were superior to other men, or simply that you were a man?"

He stared Moncin straight in the face, sternly, and the man nearly fell backward, taking his chair with him.

"Because, ever since there have been men in the world, murder has always been regarded as the greatest of all crimes, and there are people who consider that it must take exceptional courage.

"I suppose the first time, on February 2nd, it brought you relief, a momentary intoxication.

"You'd taken your precautions, for you didn't wish to pay the price, to go to the scaffold, to prison, or to some lunatic asylum.

"You are a middle-class criminal, Monsieur Moncin, a mollycoddle of a criminal, a criminal who must have his comforts and his little attentions.

"That is why, ever since I set eyes on you, I have been tempted to employ the methods for which the police are so often blamed. You are afraid of being hit, afraid of physical pain.

"If I hit you across the face with the back of my hand you would collapse; and who knows whether you wouldn't choose to confess, for fear of being hit again."

Maigret must, unintentionally, have been terrible in the anger that had gradually taken possession of him; for Moncin had shrunk into himself and his face was ashen.

"Don't be afraid. I'm not going to hit you. In fact I'm even wondering whether it's you I'm really angry with.

"You proved yourself to be clever. You chose a district where you knew every hole and corner, as only those brought up in a place can know it.

"You chose a weapon which was silent and which at the same time gave you a feeling of physical satisfaction as you used it. It wouldn't have been the same to pull the trigger of a revolver, or to pour some poison.

"You had to have some furious, violent gesture. You needed to destroy and to feel that you were destroying.

"Just to strike the blow was not enough; you had to go on and on afterward, like an angry little boy.

"You tore your victim's dress and underclothes, and the psychiatrists will no doubt see something symbolic in that.

"You didn't rape your victims because you're not capable of that, because you've never been a real man."

Moncin suddenly raised his head and glared at Maigret clenching his teeth; he looked ready to tear his eyes out.

"Those dresses, slips, bras, and panties were just so many female attributes that you were tearing to pieces.

"What I'm wondering now is whether one of those two women suspected you, not necessarily the first time, but later.

"When you went to Montmartre, didn't you tell your wife you were going to see your mother?

"Didn't she make the connection between the crimes and those visits of yours?

"You know, Monsieur Moncin, I shall remember you all my life, because never before in my career has a case bothered me so much, taken so much out of me.

"When you were arrested, yesterday, neither of those women thought you were innocent.

"And one of them decided to save you.

"If it was your mother, she had only a few steps to go, to get to Rue de Maistre.

"If it was your wife, that implies that, on the assumption we should release you, she was prepared to spend her life married to a killer.

"I do not reject either hypothesis. The two women have been here since the early hours of this morning, face to face in an office, and neither of them has uttered a word.

"The one who has committed murder knows what she did.

"The one who is innocent knows that the other is not, and I wonder if she doesn't feel a secret jealousy.

"For years they've been competing to prove which of them loved you the most, which of them possessed you most completely.

"And how could either possess you more completely than by saving your neck?"

The telephone interrupted him as he was about to continue.

"Hello! . . . Yes, it's me . . . Yes, sir . . . He's here . . . I beg your pardon, but I need him for an hour longer . . . No, the papers were telling the truth . . . An hour! . . . They're both at the Quai. . . ."

He rang off impatiently, and went and opened the door of the inspectors' office.

"Bring me those two women."

He felt an urge to get it over. If the attack he had just launched did not bring him to the goal, he realized he would not be able to settle the case.

He had asked for only an hour, not because he was sure of himself, but as a kind of petition. In an hour's time he would throw in his hand and Coméliau could do as he chose.

"Come in, ladies."

His rage was betrayed only by a kind of vibration in his voice, by the exaggerated calm of some of his movements, such as when he pulled a chair forward for each of them.

"I will not try to deceive you. Shut the door, Janvier. No, don't go away. Stay here and take notes. As I said, I will not try to deceive you, to make you think Moncin has confessed. I might have questioned you separately. As you see, I have decided not to resort to the usual police stratagems."

Moncin's mother, who had refused to sit down, strode over to him, her mouth open, and he said sharply:

"Be quiet! Not now . . ."

Yvonne Moncin was sitting quietly on the edge of her chair, like a young lady paying a call. She had glanced at her husband, without lingering, and was now staring at the superintendent as though, not content with listening to him, she was trying to read his lips.

"Whether he confesses or not, he has committed five murders, and you know it, both of you, for you know his weaknesses better than anyone. Sooner or later it will be proved. Sooner or later he will end up in prison or in an asylum.

"One of you got it in her head that by committing another murder she could avert suspicion from him.

"All that remains is for us to find out which of you, last night, killed a certain Jeanine Laurent at the corner of Rue de Maistre."

Moncin's mother at last had a chance to speak.

"You have no right to question us with no lawyer present. I forbid them to speak, either of them. It is our right to have legal advice."

"Kindly sit down, Madame, unless you have a confession to make."

"That's the last straw—to suggest I should make a confession! You are behaving like . . . like a boor, which is what you are, and you . . . you . . ."

During the hours she had spent alone with her daughter-in-law she had been silently assembling so many resentful thoughts that she had now lost the power to express them.

"I tell you once again to sit down. If you continue to make a scene I shall have you taken away by an inspector who will question you while I deal with your son and daughter-in-law."

This prospect suddenly calmed her down. The change took place from one second to the next. She stood for an instant with her mouth open in stupefaction, and then she seemed to be retorting:

"I'd like to see you do that!"

Wasn't she his mother? Weren't her rights more long-standing, more self-evident, than those of a chit her son just happened to have married?

It wasn't Yvonne who had put him into the world, it was she.

"Not only," Maigret resumed, "did one of you hope to save Moncin by committing a crime similar to his while he was locked up, but that one, I am convinced, had known for a long time what was going on. So she had the courage to remain alone with him day after day, in the same room, with no protection, with no chance of escape if he should suddenly have the idea of killing her too.

"That one loved him enough, in her own way, to . . ."

The glance Madame Moncin threw at her daughter-in-law did not escape him. Never, perhaps, had he read such hatred in a human eye.

As for Yvonne, she had not flickered an eyelash. Holding her red morocco bag with both hands, she continued to stare at Maigret as though hypnotized, not missing one expression that passed over his face.

"It only remains for me to tell you that Moncin will almost certainly save his head. The psychiatrists, as usual, will not agree about him, they will argue in front of a jury who will not understand what it is all about, and there is every chance that he will get the benefit of the doubt, in which case he will be sent to spend the rest of his days in an asylum."

The man's lips quivered. What was he thinking of at that precise moment? He must be horribly afraid of the guillotine, and afraid of prison as well. But wasn't he now conjuring up the picture of a lunatic asylum as the popular imagination sees such places?

Maigret felt convinced that if he could be promised a room to himself, a nurse, the latest thing in treatment, and the attention of some distinguished specialist, he would not hesitate to talk.

"For the woman, it isn't the same thing. For six months, Paris has been living in terror, and people never forgive those who have frightened them. The members of the jury will be Parisians, the fathers or husbands of women who might have been stabbed to death by Moncin at some street corner.

"There will be no question of madness.

"In my opinion it is the woman who will pay.

"She knows that.

"It is one or the other of you.

"One or the other of you, to save a man, or, more precisely, in order to preserve what she regards as her property, has risked her neck."

"I am perfectly willing to die for my son," said Madame Moncin, suddenly and distinctly. "He is my child. It does not matter to me what he has done. It doesn't matter to me what becomes of the little tarts who walk the streets of Montmartre at night."

"You killed Jeanine Laurent?"

"I do not know her name."

"You are responsible for the murder committed on Rue de Maistre last night?"

She hesitated, looked at Moncin, and finally said "Yes."

"In that case, can you tell me the color of the victim's dress?"

This was a detail Maigret had asked the press not to make public.

"I . . . It was too dark to . . ."

"Excuse me! You are aware that she was set upon less than five yards away from a street lamp . . ."

"I didn't pay attention."

"But when you slashed the material . . ."

The crime had been committed more than fifty yards away from the nearest street lamp.

In the ensuing silence Yvonne Moncin's voice was heard to say calmly, like a schoolgirl in class:

"The dress was blue."

She was smiling, she had not moved; now she turned to stare defiantly at her mother-in-law.

In her own mind, didn't she consider she had won the match?

"Yes, it was blue," sighed Maigret, at last allowing his nerves to relax.

And the relief was so sudden, so violent, that tears came to his eyes—tears of weariness, perhaps.

"You finish it, Janvier," he muttered, getting to his feet and picking a pipe at random from the row on his desk.

Moncin's mother had sunk into herself, aged suddenly by ten years, as though her only reason for existence had been snatched from her.

Maigret did not look at Marcel Moncin, whose head had fallen forward on his chest.

The superintendent pushed through the crowd of reporters and photographers who assailed him in the corridor.

"Who was it? You know now?"

He nodded, mumbling, "Presently . . . In a few minutes . . ."

And he hurried to the little glass-paneled door that communicated with the Law Courts.

He was with the examining magistrate for only about fifteen minutes. When he came back, it was to give his orders.

"Let the mother go, of course. Coméliau wants to see the other two as soon as possible."

"Together?"

"Yes, to begin with. It's he who'll make an announcement to the press. . . ."

There was someone he would have liked to see, though not in an office and not in the corridors or the wards of an asylum: Professor Tissot, with whom he would have enjoyed a long chat such as they had had that evening in Pardon's drawing room.

He couldn't ask Pardon to arrange another dinner. And he was too tired to go to Sainte-Anne and wait till the professor could see him.

He opened the door of the inspectors' office, where all eyes turned toward him.

"It's over, boys. . . ."

He hesitated, looked around at them all, gave a weary smile, and admitted:

"Myself, I'm going to bed."

And it was true. It had seldom happened before, even when he had been up all night.

"Tell the Director . . ."

Then in the corridor, to the journalists:

"In the examining magistrate's office . . . Monsieur Coméliau will give you the particulars. . . ."

They saw him going downstairs all alone, with bowed shoulders; he stopped on the first landing and slowly lit the pipe he had just filled.

One of the drivers asked him if he wanted the car, but he shook his head.

The first thing he wanted was to go and sit on the terrace of the Brasserie Dauphine, the way he had sat for a long time on another café terrace last night.

"A pint, Superintendent?"

He looked up and replied as though ironically, with an irony intended for himself:

"Two!"

He slept till six o'clock that evening, in the damp sheets, with the window open on the Paris street noises; and when at last he appeared in the dining room, his eyes still swollen with sleep, it was in order to inform his wife:

"We're going to the movies tonight. . . ."

Arm-in-arm, as was their custom.

Madame Maigret asked him no questions. She felt, confusedly, that he had been a long way away, that he needed to get used to everyday life again, to rub shoulders with men who would restore his confidence.